NEXT CHRISTMAS
NAT CUDDINGTON

This book has 24 chapters!
If you start reading it on December 1ˢᵗ and read
one chapter a day, you will finish it on Christmas Eve!
This is not a requirement, or even a suggestion, really.
Just a fun thing that you can do if you so choose.

Other books by Nat Cuddington:

For Teens:

Arcades, Hearts, and Other Things That Break

For Adults:

Neighbourly
Turning Thirty
Between Two Worlds

NEXT CHRISTMAS

For my parents, who always made Christmas magical.

Nik

You've got to be fucking kidding me.

This is the hundredth house in a row I've been to that already has presents in all the stockings and half eaten food left out for me. Why would someone expect anyone to snack on a cookie that's already been in someone else's mouth? And I can definitely see lip marks on that glass of milk. Gross.

I catch myself sneering as I turn and face a mirror on the other side of the living room, the glow of colourful bulbs bouncing off the glass. I sigh and grab the two carrots from the table that have random bite marks taken out of them; the reindeer don't mind getting leftovers from strangers.

"Hey girls," I say as I appear back on the roof. "These people didn't leave any apples, either. I don't think people know you like them."

Rudolph whines and I tilt my head at her. "I know, sweetie. I know you like apples the best." I give her ears a rub and let out a deep breath. "This is getting really weird, isn't it?" I ask them. "It feels like the whole world is playing a prank on me."

Prancer glares at me, and I'm not sure what it means.

"What?" I ask.

She narrows her eyes and stomps her right hoof.

"I never said I was going to stop!" I say, taking a step back with my hands up in surrender. "I just said it was weird. Can I not say that things are weird?"

She twists her neck a little and tilts her head to the side.

"So you agree. It's weird." I let out a heavy sigh and hop back in the sleigh. "Well. Let's see if there are any families around here that didn't do my job for me."

There are a few houses scattered throughout the rest of the night with empty stockings and full glasses of milk, whole cookies for me, and carrots for the reindeer, which gives me some hope. I really don't understand why less and less people leave Christmas up to me every year, but I feel like there's going to be a night one year soon that every family will have done the job of Santa for me. Any houses I go into that have any sort of room in their stockings for me to add to them, I do. I add anything that will fit, even if it's a toothbrush, a clementine, or a yoyo.

I make it to one house with filled stockings and half eaten cookies, but I notice that the doll Wendy asked for isn't under the tree. All the presents are wrapped, of course, but none of them are the right size or shape, I'm sure of it. I take the doll out of my bag and place it under her stocking, so she knows that it's from me. It also isn't wrapped, so it should be a giveaway that it's not from a parent. Or maybe we should have wrapped it in wrapping paper that the parents don't have? I haven't done this in a while, now I'm getting rusty. I'll have to talk it over with the elves and see what they think is best and I'll do it next Christmas.

One house seems to have left the entire jar of milk out and I consider drinking it from that, just finishing the whole thing off, since I haven't been able to drink from the germy glasses in any of the other houses tonight, but instead I put it back in their fridge for them. Then they can have milk with their breakfast in the morning.

The next year there are even fewer houses with empty stockings, and even less that have enough room for me to add to them. Most houses have left literal crumbs of cookies, and nothing but condensation rings under empty glasses.

As the years go on, there's less and less for me to do. I wonder if people have stopped believing in me. Or maybe they think I'm dead. I have been doing this for a long time, so it makes sense that people would think that. It isn't normal for a person to live as long as I have. So that must be it. They think I've died and can no longer deliver Christmas joy, but people love Christmas joy, so they have continued the tradition on their own. Parents have been buying their own gifts for hundreds of years anyway, so that makes sense. But no, it doesn't. If they don't believe in me, or think I'm dead, why on Earth would they leave treats out for me and the reindeer? But also, why would they leave treats out and then eat it all themselves? Are they mocking me? Are they trying to tell me that they can all do my job better than I can? No, literally none of this makes sense.

I continue to travel the world every Christmas Eve and do what I can, but I feel like I'm fading away, like I'm useless. Like the world really doesn't believe in me anymore. I still manage to add something long and skinny to almost every stocking, and as the times change, the generic, please-believe-in-me gifts evolve, but they always slide in quite nicely. I actually find myself smiling in satisfaction every time a themed toothbrush, a sparkly pen, or a reusable straw grazes the fabric of the stocking and nestles cozily beside the other contents.

But one year has me losing it. Not only are all the stockings filled for me, and all the wish list presents bought, but there are wrapped presents under the tree with *my* name on the gift tag!

"From Santa?" I say out loud, picking up a present in Pokémon wrapping. I recognize the characters because every child has wanted something to do with Pokémon for Christmas the last couple of years. It has Pikachus and Charmanders playing in the snow, and they're both wearing my signature hat. "This isn't from fucking Santa! It could have been from me, but no one is letting me! Why are people pretending the presents are from me?" And then I drop the present as it hits me.

The present doesn't hit me, the realization hits me. The present hits the ground. Because I dropped it.

Have parents been pretending to be me this whole time? *The whole time?* This whole time that I've come across already filled stockings and already eaten treats they were *pretending* to be me? Why are they pretending that someone is coming into their house and leaving presents, eating their food and leaving, when there is already someone trying to do that? What is happening?

Oh no, what's happening? I can't breathe. I'm dizzy and my heart is racing and I feel like I'm going to fall over. Fall over directly into all the Pokémon themed wrapping. And that's what happens. I crash into the pile of presents with the same wrapping paper, and as I lie there trying to catch my breath, I notice the gift tags.

From Santa
From Santa
Love mom and dad

Wait a second. But they're all in the same wrapping paper. They all have the same stupid Pokémon covering them, but not all of them say they're from me. Some of them say they're from the parents. So they're pretending that half of these gifts are from me, but not pretending that I have different wrapping paper than they do? Why would I have the same goddamn wrapping paper as this family? How does that make any sense?

What is happening to the world? What is happening to me? What do people think I am?

I manage to make it back up to the roof without dying, but I panic to my reindeer, asking them what's happening to me. Of course they can't answer me, but they give me looks of reassurance. I think they're telling me that I'm not dying. I still exist. I'm here.

I'm right here. My heart is beating, albeit much too fast, but it's beating nonetheless. I'm breathing. At too rapid a pace, but I'm breathing. I can feel the air on my tongue. I feel it fill my lungs. Oh, this is helping. I grab a fistful of Blitzen's fur, and she leans into me a little, breathing on me so I know she cares. My breathing starts to slow and I feel a little better.

"I think I just had a panic attack," I say.

They all look at me as if to say, "you think?" and I can't help but chuckle. The girls are amused too, and my chuckle turns into full on roaring laughter. I almost fall over but manage to make it into the sleigh, wiping my tears that fell from laughing so hard.

"I don't know what else to do," I tell my best friend and oldest Elf, Charlie.

"Maybe you need to put something better in their stockings."

"There's no room. Literally, they're always filled tight. They have been for decades. Probably longer than that, to be honest. All I can fit in them are straw-shaped things. Or straws."

"You're putting actual straws in people's stockings?"

"Reusable straws. Colourful ones. Kids like them!"

"Okay, okay." He paces the floor a couple times and then stops. "Apple Pencils! Apple Pencils will fit! Those are straw shaped!"

"But they come in a box," I tell him.

"They come in a box when they're purchased from the Apple Store. They don't need a box if we make them. You can just slide them into every stocking and the parents will surely believe in you then! They will know for sure that they didn't just buy an Apple Pencil, take it out of the packaging, put it in their kid's stocking, and then *forget about it*. If every kid finds a mysterious Apple Pencil in their stocking on Christmas morning, you putting them there will be the only explanation!"

"You're right! Oh, this is genius! But what if they didn't get an iPad for Christmas? What if they don't have the right model to use the Apple Pencil on?"

Charlie's face lights up. "Then give them iPads too."

"What if they don't want an iPad?"

"Who doesn't want a free iPad? Nik, everyone wants a free iPad."

"Right. You're right."

"Of course I'm right."

The Apple Pencils and iPads don't work. I put one in every stocking, and for every house that doesn't obviously already have an iPad, I leave one of those too. I'm so excited, and I think for sure next year will be different. But it isn't. The next Christmas is just the same as the previous 50 or so Christmases. The stockings are filled to the brim, the food is half eaten, or there's no food at all. Presents are wrapped with my name on it, and some of the houses that got new iPads from me the previous year, now have the latest model under the tree.

I find myself aimlessly wandering through the streets, my sleigh hovering above the streetlights, waiting for me. I take a carrot nose from a snowman on someone's lawn and toss it up to the reindeer. Comet catches it and chomps down on it right away, bits of orange fluttering to the unplowed road. I go to the next house and find they also have a snowman, but this carrot is hollow and plastic. It looks like they used some snowman kit or something. Probably something they got from fake Santa last year. I take the plastic carrot anyway. It's mine now. I slip it into one of the pockets of my red coat and look up at my loyal flying friends. Well. They're not flying right now, right now they're hovering, or floating, I guess, but they do also fly. I can call them flying friends even if they aren't currently flying. What am I even going on about?

The next two Christmas Eve nights are pointless for me. I go out with my magic bag full of toys, and more Apple Pencils for some reason, but I leave almost nothing. I leave a few toys, and when I have the mental energy, I slide the odd Apple Pencil into a stocking, but I don't even know if these people want or need them. I'm just slipping them in willy nilly, because it's hard to care at this point. I've never delivered to so few houses before. I've never felt so defeated. Even the first night I really expanded my delivery radius, back when I was just Nikalaos, before this celebration was even called Christmas, I never felt like this. It was daunting then, and it felt like I had a big and hard adventure ahead of me, but tonight it just feels like there's no reward at the end. For me or anyone else. It feels like there's nothing for me to work for. I'm not making a difference at all.

I don't even go into anyone's houses because people are still awake. Houses with chimneys carry up the sounds of people talking and laughing, probably having parties while their children sleep, dreaming of getting presents from a man who isn't actually coming. I can't even show myself to the children, or the parents to tell them to stop doing my job, because time slows down so much for me on Christmas Eve, I would have to stand still for hours in order for them to see me. Instead I sit at the top of one family's chimney and listen to the quiet sounds of their talking below me. It doesn't sound like anything, really. Just tones. But they're happy tones. It might sound weird and unsettling to someone who hadn't experienced time slow like this before, but I hear it every year, and it has always calmed me. It's the only thing that I can find comfort in at this moment. The snow falling around me as if it's suspended in the air, and the sounds of happiness floating up from inside the living room. I let out a deep breath and close my eyes.

And then I head back to the North Pole, sadly I think, for the last time.

It's Christmas Eve. My former favourite day of the year, and Charlie can't get me out of bed. I don't have the energy to do anything anymore.

"Maybe I was never meant to do this forever," I say. "Maybe I was always meant to just start something, and families were always supposed to continue it on their own while I lived the rest of my normal life."

"But you didn't live a normal life. You moved to the North Pole and started aging really slowly and learned how to slow down time every Christmas Eve."

"I didn't learn how to do that. I swear I'm not the one doing it." I manage to sit up and swing my legs over the edge of the bed.

"Nik," Charlie says gently. "It's like you became one of us somehow. You didn't want to stop making people happy, and you adopted our powers."

I shrug. "And now people don't need me anymore."

"I do."

That makes me stop. I look up at him, my face tight with worry.

"I need you," Charlie says. "I've known you for longer than I haven't, and I can't imagine living another thousand years without you."

"But you could. You totally could."

He shakes his head. "That's not true. Have you looked around you lately? You adopted our powers but we also adopted the reasons you have them! We never used to celebrate Christmas and twinkle lights before you got here! And now most of us can't even remember a time before this all existed. Just because people down south don't need you anymore doesn't mean that you can't stick around! You can still stay!"

"I don't think it works like that," I say, pressing my feet to the ground and forcing myself to stand. "I think I got my powers because my intentions were so good natured. Because I brought so much joy to the world. But the world took that joy and changed it into something else. They even changed my name, and now they put that name on presents bought by someone else from a store."

"They didn't change your name, it just evolved."

I sigh. "I think my powers are going to fade away just like everything else about me."

"What if... what if we convinced people, though?"

"The Apple Pencils didn't work, Charlie," I grumble.

"I'm not talking about Apple Pencils." He's got a grin that I feel like represents an idea I'm not going to like. "I'm talking about you, going down south, and convincing people in real life. As you. Nikolaos of Myra."

"I don't think anyone talks like that anymore."

"What do you mean?"

"Never mind. What do *you* mean?"

"I mean I think you should go to a city that loves Christmas, and convince them that Santa Claus is real!"

"Yes, we've covered that. How do I do that?"

"By showing them!"

"You want me... to go South?"

"Yes!"

"How? I can't just *go South,* Charlie!"

"Why not? Oh, now that my mind is turning, I'm getting a great idea! We need someone who doesn't look like Santa to go convince everyone."

"Why does it have to be someone who doesn't look like Santa? Why can't I go?"

But Charlie is just looking at me with a grin that makes my stomach turn. He hasn't had a bad idea before, but he's also never grinned like this before.

"That's the thing," he says. "You *will* go."

"But you said the person shouldn't look like Santa, and I can't very well change my appearance, now can I?" But Charlie still has a huge grin on his face. I want to smack it off, but that's incredibly rude and unnecessary, so I don't. "Can I? Charlie, can I change my appearance?"

"Well I think I can just, age reverse you."

"Excuse me?"

"You'll still be the same age of course, and continue to age at the same rate, but you'll just look younger."

"Has this always been a power of yours? I haven't had to look like a 79-year-old man for the last fifteen hundred years?"

Charlie shakes his head and steps closer to me. "First of all, you haven't looked 79 this entire time."

I roll my eyes at him.

"I've been practicing my magic lately and seeing what all I can do," Charlie continues. "Ever since we've started trying to get people to believe in you, I've been seeing how far I can take it." He pauses as if he's afraid to tell me what his plan is. He closes his eyes and takes a deep breath before speaking again. "I think I can make you look like a respectable 36-year-old human man."

"Wait, what? You can? And 36? Why 36?"

"Well, give or take a few years. Approximately 36."

"Okay, why?"

"I feel like that's a good age. Don't you think that's a good age?"

"I don't know, I was 36 like a billion years ago."

"I just think that the people you will have to convince are families with young children, and most parents with young children are in their thirties."

"Yes," I say slowly, thinking back on some Christmas wishes I've listened to over the last several years. "Parents do seem to be getting older these days."

"So what I'm getting at," Charlie continues, "is I can make you look like not Santa, so you can go to a town that's not The North Pole, to convince people that Santa is real."

"Okay so my next question is why can't I look like me? If I'm trying to convince people that I'm real, shouldn't I look like me? I've seen the ads and billboards and stuff everyone makes with me on them. I mean, we don't look exactly the same, but the resemblance is certainly there."

"No. Absolutely not." Charlie shakes his head, and now I'm just confused. "Everyone's belief in you has evolved to something strange, and people may or may not be pretending to be you. I mean you said there were presents wrapped that said they were from Santa, right? Either way, they don't believe in you the way they're supposed to. So if you go around looking like Santa, looking like the Santa in those ads you've seen, and telling people that you're Santa, everyone is going to think that you're mentally unstable."

"I don't know what that means."

"They'll think you're having some kind of delusional episode."

I blink at him. "Really?"

He sighs. "Yes. I mean, probably. So they'll think that, or they'll think that you're also pretending and simply won't believe you."

"So you're saying that I should go to a town that's not the North Pole, looking not like Santa, and what? What am I supposed to do?"

"That part I'm not entirely sure of. And this might have to be a multi-year project."

I cover my face with my hands and whine. "Charlie," I say, dragging his name out. "A multi-year project to convince people that I'm trying to give their kids presents that you have no idea how to execute sounds like a terrible idea."

"I think you can do it. You have a certain charm."

"Do I?"

"Of course you do! You're Santa! And you're literally magic. So I think if you talk to the right people, they'll feel the magic too. And then it'll spread and it'll be just like old times before you know it."

"So you just want me to talk?" I ask.

He shrugs. "Yeah. Make friends."

"I don't know how to make friends!"

"Am I not your friend?"

"You've been my friend for longer than most things have even existed, Charlie."

"Okay, but you're friends with literally everyone in The North Pole."

"I wouldn't say I'm friends with *everyone*, we just all know each other. And of course everyone knows who *I* am up here, so it's easier! Plus it took so long for me to get close with everyone and I don't have that kind of time now. I haven't made any new friends in about a thousand years; I don't know how any of that works!"

"Somehow I think it'll come to you. You're a natural."

"It's Christmas Eve, Charlie, what am I supposed to do tonight?"

"You could still go out, but I honestly don't think it'll make a difference."

I wince at that. "Great."

"Sorry," he says. "I didn't mean it in a bad way. Why don't you have a good rest tonight, and we'll start planning in the morning."

"This feels weird. I can't not go out."

"You're telling me you weren't already planning on staying here this year? You were curled up in bed like a dying cat, and now you're telling me that you can't not go out?"

"I don't know!" I half-yell. "I'm confused!"

"I think we should start planning Operation Santa tonight."

"Please don't call it that."

"What would you like to call it?"

"Nothing. The plan to get me back."

"Excellent. Instead of delivering non-presents tonight, I think we should start planning Operation Plan to get you Back."

"Stop trying to give it a name and we can start planning it."

"Excellent."

CHAPTER 3

We planned Operation Get Santa Back, or whatever Charlie's been calling it lately, and then waited 11 months to get it started. It's now the end of November and I look just like I did when I was in my thirties, and it's weirding me out. I decided to keep a closely trimmed beard, because I like that there's a little bit of grey sprinkled throughout it. The rest of my hair is dark, with just a bit of grey around my temples, and if it wasn't for that I might look even younger than Charlie does. Hmm, my nose is definitely smaller. Did my nose used to be smaller when I was younger? It's not as round on the end, but I guess I still look like me. Charlie has dressed me in a pair of dark denim pants that fit over my thighs and calves with just enough room for them to not be tight, but not be 'skinny jeans' as he called them, and a red hooded sweatshirt. I'm not sure about my green shoes; they seem to have zero waterproofing and zero arch support, but Charlie said people wouldn't ask for them for Christmas all the time if they weren't cool. I suppose I have to agree with him. I've got a bag packed with more clothes and according to Charlie, my furniture is going to make it to my apartment. I don't know how he's getting furniture to an apartment in small town Ontario Canada, but I'm not asking any more questions.

"Oh, you might need to rent a car once you're settled, so I made this Ontario Driver's Handbook for you in the workshop. I'm pretty sure it's the same as the real one," Charlie says, handing me a floppy paperback.

"Oh," I reply, looking at it. "So if I read this book then I'll know how to drive a car?"

"I think so."

I shrug and put it in my bag. "Okay. Thanks."

The next few days are an exhausting blur. I go from plane to plane and sleep in uncomfortable plastic airport chairs, try to sleep in narrow airplane seats, and keep getting distracted by children pointing at me and smiling. Why are they pointing at me and smiling? I see one little girl whisper something to her mom from across the aisle of my last plane and she shushes her and tells her she's being rude. I have no idea what's going on, but all I can think of is how she wants a blue mountain bike for Christmas. She'll probably get one. Whether it's the exact one that she's been dreaming of is another question, but I'm sure her parents will at least get her a bike. A blue one, even. If I wasn't taking this year off I would get her the one she wanted, even if there was already one sitting beside the Christmas tree when I got there. Just to spite her parents. No one can do my job better than I can.

As we're getting off and making our way down the suspended hallway thing that brings us into the airport, that same little girl grabs onto my hand. I look down at her and smile, but I don't close my fingers around hers. Something is telling me that I shouldn't.

"Are you Santa?" she asks me.

My heart stammers and I take in a breath. Have children been smiling and pointing at me because they can feel my magic? Do they all know who I am?

I crouch down to her level and give her a warm smile. "What makes you think I'm Santa?" I ask her.

People walk around us but no one seems to be annoyed with us standing in the middle of the walkway. Maybe they think I'm her dad and I'm comforting her about something that's upset her.

"I don't know," she says with a shrug.

"Caroline, what did I say?" her mother says, grabbing her arm.

"It's okay," I tell her mom, looking up at her.

"No, it's not. Thank you for being kind, but she needs to learn her manners." Caroline lets go of my hand as her mom drags her away, but she looks back at me for as long as she can. Watching her little face turned back to me the whole time reminds me of when I delivered presents back in Germany and the Netherlands. Children would put their boots beside their fireplaces, or outside their doors for me to fill, and sometimes I would catch them spying on me through the window. This was before I had any magic of course, so they were able to do so, and seeing their faces in the corner of the windows as I approached always made me smile. I knew they thought I couldn't see them, and I would pretend not to, but it warmed my heart to see them so excited, and to see them crouch below the window as I got closer, their fingers still gripping the sill. I see their expressions in Caroline's face as she gets further and further away from me, and I'm suddenly so homesick. Homesick for a time, and for a feeling, instead of a place. I keep my crouched position and let people continue to walk around me until Caroline and her mom are lost in the crowd. I let out a deep breath and stand up again, hoping this crashing wave of grief won't last much longer. That's when I realize I left my bag on the plane.

"I'm sorry, I can't let anyone back on the plane," the flight attendant says to me.

"But I left my bag," I say. "I just realized that I don't have it."

"You can claim it at lost luggage."

"But it's not lost, it's literally still on the plane. This plane right here."

Another flight attendant comes up behind her, a boy, maybe the age of 21, and whose name I know to be Justin, smiles at me. "What seat row was it above? I'll get it for you."

"Thank you, I really appreciate it." I tell him where I was sitting and he leaves without another word. I smile at the first flight attendant who is still standing guard at the door, but she doesn't smile back. When the boy comes back, he holds the bag out to me and I take it from him. He wants a PS5 for Christmas.

"I hope you have a wonderful holiday," he says.

"Thanks, you too. I hope you get everything you asked for."

The girl flight attendant, whose name I know is Rachel, looks at us with a judging expression, as if we're out of line, or weird for saying what we're saying to each other.

The boy, Justin, smiles in a way that seems innocent and pure, reminding me of a person who had just been given a compliment from someone who means a lot to them. I nod my head at him and turn back towards the airport.

Maybe this won't be so hard after all.

I manage to get an airport taxi to take me the rest of the way, but the town I'm going to is almost two hours away and it's late by the time I make it to my apartment. It's a cute two-story walk-up with little mailboxes when you first enter. The stairs have a rubber coating on top and my wet boots squeak on them as I make my way up to the second floor. All the doors have numbers on them and from the ones I can see once I exit the stairwell, I know that I have to turn right down the hall to find my apartment. It's all the way at the end, and just as I approach the door, the one across the hall opens. A lady about my age – er, the age I'm currently supposed to be portraying, steps into the hall and flips a dark braid of hair over her shoulder. She's got her hair in two braids, tied at the end with bright blue elastics. I guess one of the braids had fallen over her shoulder and it was bugging her or something. She smiles at me, but it's tight, sort of forced. Like she's stressed but still wants to be polite. Her name is Morgan and she wants a boyfriend for Christmas. Oh. Is she aware that's not the sort of thing you can ask

Santa for? I'm sure she knows she can't ask Santa for a boyfriend. We can't very well make people in my workshop, let alone ones that will for sure love the person who asked for them.

"I'm just moving in," I say.

"Welcome to the building," she says quickly. I watch her walk down the hall and then I open the door to my new place.

All my furniture is set up. I don't have a way to contact Charlie to ask him how he did it, but I make a mental note to ask him the next time I'm home. Whenever that'll be. It's November twenty-sixth, so maybe I have enough time to convince people that I exist before Christmas. Christmas eve would be ideal. I really don't want to have to be here for longer than that, let alone multiple years. I don't know what to do with myself, so I go to bed.

The next morning, I decide to go out for breakfast and get some waffles. I've never had waffles that weren't made by elves or myself before, so I think that would be a delightful treat. But when I get closer to the door that leads into the hall of the building, I hear screaming. Like, blood curdling screams that make me stop in my tracks. I feel frozen for a second, and then almost as quickly as it started, I can move again. I open the door to see a small child on the dirty floor, kicking her dad in the shins and screaming, "But Auntie Morgan takes me! Auntie Morgan takes me!"

"Olivia," her dad says with a calm tone. "I told you your Auntie Morgan has to work this morning. She has a very important meeting. But I like taking you to school, don't you like it when I take you to school?"

"No!" Olivia screams at him. "You don't do it right!"

How can someone not take their kid to school right? What is involved in taking a child to school? This is when her dad, Brett, notices me. He winces as if he's embarrassed, and then nods at me. I nod back, but am afraid to leave the scene. I'm not sure what I'm supposed to do in a situation like this, and I don't want to be rude.

"Olivia, I understand that you're upset, but we have to get going or you're going to be late."

"NO!" Olivia screams.

"If you don't get off the floor right now, I'm calling Santa on the phone and telling him how bad you're being."

I'm sorry, what? He's going to call me? How does he have my number? Wait, what am I saying? I don't even have a phone. He can't call me. Why is he lying about calling me? Why would a parent call me, anyway? And I thought people didn't believe in me anymore. Unless he's just taking this pretending thing too far?

"NO!" Olivia screams again, but I have a feeling it's in response to her dad calling, um, me, apparently, and not about getting to school anymore.

"I have his number saved in my contacts, Livvy." Brett takes out his cell phone – I really should get one of those – and presses the screen so that it lights up. "I talk to him all the time about you, and he is going to be so disappointed that you're behaving like this, especially in front of our new neighbour."

Why would I care how a child I don't know has been acting? I mean I suppose it's embarrassing for people to be told about your subpar behaviour, but that's not what I'm getting from this threat.

Olivia looks up at me and gasps. She wipes the tears off her cheeks and stands up. She's looking at me like she's mortified that I've witnessed her having a tantrum.

"Is he… Is he really going to call Santa?" she asks me, her bottom lip trembling a little.

I shrug my shoulders. "Um, I don't know," I say. "I don't know your dad, so I don't know."

"Have *you* called Santa before?"

I don't know what to say. I can't tell her that I haven't called Santa, because I'm Santa, and I can't very well call myself, but I don't know how to back Brett up. First I need to understand why he would even want to call me and why he would lie about it, and I also need to know if other people are involved in this lie. Does he tell his daughter that he's the only one who talks to Santa on the phone, or is Olivia under the impression that all parents talk to Santa on the phone?

For clarification, I talk to zero parents on the phone. Like I said, I don't even have a phone.

I look to Brett for a little help, and he sort of nods at me, and opens his eyes wider as if to say… something. I don't know what he's trying to tell me. I look back at Olivia and stammer.

"I don't have children," I tell her.

"So?" she says.

"Let's go, sweetie," Brett says. Olivia huffs but doesn't protest this time, and the two of them walk down the hall. I let them get to the stairs before I start to leave, and I try not to notice Olivia looking back at me every few feet with a curious expression on her face. I don't want her asking me questions about Santa again.

She wants an iPhone for Christmas, by the way.

I find a cute little breakfast place on a fairly lonely stretch of road while I'm out for a walk to explore the town. It's a bit of a ways from the main part of town, but the walk here only took about forty minutes. It's been nice because the cars aren't very frequent, and the driveways attach to houses that are far back from the road, almost hidden in the trees. It would have been an even nicer walk if my toes weren't so cold. It's a good thing it isn't snowing or they'd probably also be wet. I make a mental note to tell Charlie these shoes are only good for warmer weather, and to wear a pair of boots the next time I go out. The restaurant is set back from the road much like the houses in this area of town, and I smile as I approach, excited to eat in a regular restaurant. And for my toes to warm up.

The server, Amber, brings my banana and Nutella waffles over with a smile and also gives me a pitcher of maple syrup, which I very much appreciate. The waffles are delightful. The ones I make at home are fluffier, but for waffles made without magic, I'd say they're pretty good. Very good, actually. I end up getting a second helping, and my server thinks I'm joking at first and laughs at me as she takes my plate away. But when she comes over with my bill, I tell her that I wasn't kidding around and that I could eat them all day if I had enough room. But I do have room for another plate. She laughs again but does bring me more and I eat these ones slowly, savouring the sweetness and nice combination of crispy outside and warm, fluffy inside.

"Can I ask you a question?" Amber asks as she brings me my new bill.

"Of course," I say.

"Are you famous?"

"Am I famous?" I repeat, confused.

"Yeah. Like, are you in movies, or in a TV show I would have seen?"

"Not that I'm aware of."

"Oh. It just feels like I know you from somewhere, but I haven't seen you around before."

"Yeah, I get that a lot, actually. I guess I just have one of those faces."

"Must be."

"Can I ask *you* a question?"

She raises her eyebrows at me. "Sure."

"What do you want for Christmas?" I know what she wants for Christmas. But I just want to hear it from her. I haven't heard anyone actually confirm if I've been right this whole time.

"Oh. Hmm." She looks up a little as if she's thinking about her answer. "I don't know. My hair straightener's getting pretty old. Maybe a new hair straightener."

"Hmm." Is she lying or have I lost my touch?

She smirks at me. "You don't sound pleased with my answer."

"Oh, I was just expecting you to say something else is all."

"Yeah?"

"Yeah." I stand up and take money out of my wallet that Charlie provided me with. "Is it customary to leave a tip in this region?"

"Yes?"

"Perfect. You did a great job, I really appreciate everything you did for me this morning." I hand her enough money to cover the bill and about a thirty percent tip, and she smiles as she takes it.

"Thank you so much."

"Of course." I smile and head to the door, but before I get a chance to open it, Amber calls after me.

"A light saber," she says.

I almost collapse in relief, but instead I turn around and face her. "I'm sorry?" I say.

"I actually want a light saber for Christmas," she clarifies. "One of the expensive ones that light up and make noises when you swing them and hit things. I know it's nerdy, but that's what I want."

"What colour?" I ask.

"Yellow."

"I'll do my best."

She scrunches her face at me, most likely confused, but then she almost gasps, and smiles. Like she's finally placed me. I smile back and turn to leave.

Is this all I need to do to make people believe in me? Everyone seems to recognize me even if they don't know who I am. I think all I have to do is do a little subtle magic like this in a few towns, and then word will spread, and I'll be back to doing my job in no time. December will come and parents will only buy the presents that will have their names on the tag, and they'll leave Santa's presents to me. Maybe I can figure out why people are pretending to be me, while I'm at it. It makes sense that parents would get the presents for their kids that I'm supposed to get them if they don't believe in me, but it doesn't make sense for them to get presents for their kids and then pretend they're from someone else.

I see a sign for a car rental place on my walk home so I decide to stop in and pick one up. If I want to go anywhere outside of town, having a car will be much easier. When I walk up to the counter inside and ask about renting a car, the lady working smiles at me and asks for my licence.

"Oh. My licence?" I ask.

"Yes. Your driver's licence?"

"Oh. Yes, I definitely have one of those." I read about them in the driving handbook that Charlie made me. I read all about the rules of the road as well, so I think I'm good to go. I pull out my wallet and grab the blue plastic card with my picture on it, and hand it to her.

She smiles as she takes it and types some things into her computer. I pay her a deposit and she hands me the keys to my newly rented car. How exciting! I find it in the parking lot and press the little button with a picture of an open lock, and see the lights flash, telling me that it's unlocked and I can now enter. I get in the car and put my seatbelt on, and then I look around, feeling a little lost. I'm actually, uh, not sure how to turn it on. There's no on button on the key thingy the lady gave me, and there's no on button anywhere on the car. I look at the steering wheel, and around it, and then I find a key hole under it to the right-hand side. I stick the key in and turn it, and the car makes a noise and rumbles beneath me!

"Okay," I say to myself, "brake on the left, go on the right." I find the gear shifter and move the stick from P to D and slowly press my foot into the gas pedal. The car lurches forward so I slam my foot onto the brake, and the car jolts as it stops. I take a deep breath and try again, pressing the gas more gently this time. It eases forward much nicer and I manage to make a circle around the parking lot before coming to a stop at the road. Okay. I can do this. I can drive a car. I read a book on it, and I can drive a freakin' magical sleigh, so this should be a piece of cake.

I drive around town to get the feel for this big piece of machinery that I'm in control of, and after about an hour of turning through the same streets and signalling at the same intersections, I think I start to get the hang of it. I go out the next day to practice some more, and by the day after that, I feel confident enough to leave town, so I decide to go to Costco. I've heard it's all the rage, and I'm quite curious to check it out.

But what I see once I'm there completely gobsmacks me. There are boxes upon boxes of little Elf dolls. The package says it's called Gingerbread Elf, and explains that they're a tradition from Susan's family, whoever that is, and that she wants everyone else to experience the *Gingerbread Magic* just as her family did. What the hell is Gingerbread Magic? And why is it in italics? The box says that they're Santa's helpers from the North Pole and they watch over the kids throughout December to make sure they're behaving. I don't see what elves have to do with children behaving and why I need to know about it. And if they're from the North Pole, why the hell are they in a box? And why do they have to be purchased? And why is it a shitty little doll? Elves aren't even short, let alone miniature! I mean, some of them are short, like all people. They come in all shapes, sizes, and colours. But they most certainly do not come in a box. And none of them wear ugly brown outfits like these ones here are wearing! I need to get to the bottom of why everyone seems to simultaneously believe and not believe in me. Also who is Susan? Where did her Elf come from and why is she selling hundreds of them to people at Costco? It's starting to make my head spin. I pick up a boxed "elf" and throw it my cart. For research. I also grab a nice fake Christmas Tree with pre-installed lights, and a big pumpkin pie.

A few people smile at me as I pass them, as if I'm an acquaintance they want to acknowledge but not necessarily catch up with. The checkout line goes quickly and I put my card back in my wallet, wondering how Charlie got it. With magic, I suppose, the same way he and the other elves make toys. But he's been doing a lot more of that lately, and I'm worried he's going to wear himself out.

I'd been eyeing the hot food area as I waited in line, and now that I've paid for my things, I decide to give the food a try. I get a poutine and a hotdog, and take a seat at one of the tables. The poutine is pretty good, although I've had better, but the hotdog is magnificent. It's big and juicy, and has a very satisfying snap when I bite into it. I smother it in yellow mustard and nod at people who seem to be staring. They nod back or smile, and some people with children almost walk over to me, only to be stopped by their parents. One kid breaks free of her parent's hold though, and races over to me, her little legs going as fast as they can.

"I want a playdough kitchen," she says, her words sounding like her tongue is too big for her mouth.

"That sounds like a great gift idea," I say to her.

"Riley, what did I say?" her dad says, coming over to her and gently grabbing her arm. Then he looks at me. "I'm so sorry."

"It's no bother." I wave him off and smile.

"I don't want this to sound rude, but she insisted that you were Santa Claus. Which makes no sense, because you obviously look nothing like Santa."

I laugh a little, because I do in fact, look exactly like Santa, just a younger version of him. Er, of me. "I've been getting that a lot, lately. I'm not sure why."

"You must radiate Christmas Joy."

"Well I do try to," I say, nodding at the Christmas tree in my cart.

"Enjoy the rest of your meal," he says. "And sorry again."

"It's not a problem. Have a merry Christmas, Riley."

"You too!" she says, grabbing her dad's hand as they walk away.

I finish my meal without being interrupted again, but I can't stop thinking about Riley and her dad. Riley could somehow tell that I'm Santa, and her dad even seemed to believe in me even though he didn't realize who he was talking to. My head starts to hurt thinking about it, so I take my empty food wrappers to the garbage and make my way to the exit.

"How old's your kid?" the receipt checker asks me at the door.

"Hmm?" I ask. Why do they think I have a kid?

"The Elf. That for your kid?"

"Oh. Um. Yes. Of course."

"Is this their first elf?"

I look behind me to see if we're holding up a line, but of course there's no one else waiting, so it would be rude of me not to answer. "Yes, it's my first elf. I don't really understand it, to be honest."

"Oh, your kid is going to love it. You might not, but I guarantee you, they will think it's the most magical thing ever."

"I'm sorry, why won't I like it?"

He laughs a little and then nods behind me, where a lineup is now forming, so now that I actually want to talk to this person, I have to leave. Why did he laugh? What's funny? Why wouldn't I like it?

I rip the elf package open as soon as I get into my apartment and find a book inside which tells a short and vague story of the Gingerbread Elves. Gingerbread Elves are not a thing, but apparently this doll is a Gingerbread Elf. I skim through it, and the back of the book has a little envelope with a folded adoption certificate inside. I think I'm supposed to write the Elf's name on it. How am I supposed to know what its name is? And why would the adoption certificate come *folded* and stuffed in an envelope? It's going to have creases all over it!

"What's your name?" I ask it. It's still inside the box, his arms bent and rubber hands on his hips. "Are you alive? Who made you? Because my elves sure didn't. Is there another Santa around? Getting to the houses before me and stealing everyone's wrapping paper? Does this other Santa have Gingerbread Elves? Tell me!" Instead of answering, it stares off to the side with a sly smile like it's thinking about all the trouble it's going to get into, and I shiver. It gives me the creeps.

I finally decide to take it out of the box and set it free. I have to find a pair of scissors because the elf doll is attached to the box with plastic restraints. He's wearing a brown outfit that's lined with multicoloured felt sprinkles and white trim that I think is supposed to be icing. Ah, I get it, he's dressed like a gingerbread man. His little floppy hat that seems to be attached to his head is like mine, only it's brown where mine is red.

I finally get the doll out and squeal as its legs unfold. They are much too long for its body and the knee joints are not in a natural spot. Also instead of feet, it has a set of bright pink balls. Why are there balls where there should be feet? How are they supposed to keep their balance with ball feet? I set it on the table and watch it for a good five minutes, but nothing happens. Maybe I was supposed to name it first. Maybe I should read the damn book.

Yeah, so I think I'm supposed to name it. Like I observed when I skimmed through it, the story is not very detailed and doesn't give me much information about how this whole thing works. It rhymes though, which is fun, and the illustrations are wonderful. The book says that its mission of spying on children - which, can we all admit is creepy and weird? – won't start until you name your friend. Which doesn't make sense to me at all. It's either your friend or a spy, but it definitely can't be both. And not being able to spy on you until it has a name is also a preposterous idea.

This is so silly.

"Okay," I say out loud, putting my hands on my hips. "What should your name be?"

It continues to stare off to the side as if it doesn't care about my existence.

"I'll name you Charlie, after my best friend."

Still nothing happens. Do I have to write his name on the creased certificate? I sigh and look for a pen. There's no pen in the entire apartment. Now I have to go back out to buy a pen. For fuck's sakes. I grab my keys, slip my boots on, and put on my coat. As soon as I step into the hall, I gasp, because someone is coming out of the apartment across from me and it startles me.

"Oh my god," she says, putting a hand on her chest. I guess she was startled too.

"Sorry. Weird timing."

"Yeah," she laughs. "Sorry, we sort of met the other day, but I didn't introduce myself. I'm Morgan."

Of course I knew her name the first time I met her, but I can't tell her that. I can't tell her that there's a magic that exists inside me that allows me to know what everyone's name is and what they want for Christmas. Surely I can't tell her that. Right? So instead I say, for some reason, "Ah. That makes sense."

She scrunches her nose in confusion. "What makes sense?"

"Oh. Just a few days ago. Two people were in the hall talking about you and now here you are. You're Morgan."

"They were talking about me, eh? What were they saying?"

"That you're better at taking Olivia to school."

She laughs out loud. "That's hilarious."

We stand and smile at each other for longer than is probably necessary and then I realize that I haven't told her my name. I take in a surprised sounding breath and stick out my hand to shake.

"I'm Nik," I say.

"Nice to meet you, Nik," she says as she shakes my hand.

"You too."

"I don't live here, but I'm here a lot, so you'll probably see more of me."

"Oh, cool." I want to say that I'm looking forward to it, but I believe that's creepy, so I leave that thought in my head.

"Well I need to get going," she says, pointing her thumb down the hall.

"Yeah, me too. I need to buy a pen."

"You need to buy a pen?"

"Yes."

"Just one?"

"Yes. I need to put an elf name on a piece of paper."

"A Gingerbread Elf?" she asks.

"Yes. Do you know about them?"

"Everyone knows about them. Do you not know about them?"

I shake my head. "This is my first time."

"Oh dear. Well, I have a pen." She opens the bag on her shoulder and rummages through it for a couple seconds and produces a white pen with blue writing on it. I take it from her and examine it.

"Big Bay Point Dentistry," I say, reading the blue writing aloud.

She just shrugs and smiles.

"Do you have a minute?" I ask. "I'll write the name out and give it back."

"Don't be silly, you can keep it."

"Is this pen important?"

"It's a dentist pen."

"Yes."

She narrows her eyes at me and then smirks.

"Are dentist pens not important?" I ask.

She giggles a little. "You're funny. Enjoy your elf. And let me know if you run out of ideas. I can get pretty creative with Olivia's."

"Ideas?" I ask.

She laughs again and waves as she heads down the hall.

Seriously, what is happening, and what is with these elves? Why does everyone but me know about them? I need to find out more about this Susan person, since she's the one who told everyone about it. Maybe it's her fault that everyone already has their presents by the time I get to their houses to deliver them.

I take the pen inside and open the certificate. I write in Myra for the family name, put today's date, and then write my Gingerbread Elf's name. Charlie. I put the pen down and step back.

"There," I say. "It's official. You have a name, so you have gingerbread magic now. I think. You can move."

He's still staring off to the side. Not moving.

"Move!" I say, getting frustrated. "I don't know what else I'm supposed to do!" Apparently, it's supposed to go to the North Pole at night and for some reason report to *me* but this has literally never happened. Are millions of elves dressed in stupid cookie costumes really supposed to visit me every single night telling me about a child's behaviour? That's madness! And not to mention impossible. I mean, I am magic, but let's be realistic here. I deliver presents all over the world, or, used to deliver presents all over the world in one night because time slows down around me on Christmas Eve. Time can't slow down *every* night for the month of December just so floppy little elf dolls can come tell me if all the kids are being good or bad. Also why do I need to know if kids have been good or bad? Do people think I only bring presents to well-behaved children? Is that why Brett said he was going to call me to tell me about Olivia's behaviour? Is this like, a thing?

I wish my reindeer could have brought me here. If they were able to bring me here then I would be able to get home and talk to Charlie. If I want to go home now, it's going to be a giant pain in my ass. That's probably why Charlie had me take a zillion planes to get here, instead of figuring out if there was a way for my girls to fly outside of Christmas eve. For the very reason that he knew I would find any excuse to get back to the North Pole instead of staying here and figuring this all out.

"Damn you, Charlie," I say out loud, looking up at the ceiling, as if that's the direction of the North Pole. And then I look at my new doll, since I've named him Charlie, to see if he reacted to me swearing at him. Of course he hasn't moved a millimetre.

Plus I already know the reindeer don't have the magic to fly all year round. I was just upset and homesick, and said things in my head that I didn't mean.

The next morning, I get up to find Charlie the floppy Gingerbread Elf doll still lying on my kitchen table. It didn't go to the North Pole and it certainly didn't get into any mischief while I was sleeping! I wonder if I can ask Morgan about it. She said to ask her if I needed help with ideas, which I don't think is the same thing, but maybe she can still help me. I think about it all day and finally decide in the afternoon to go knock on her brother's door and see if she's there.

I'm nervous, and I run my fingers through my hair as I step into the hall. I'm allowed to knock on his door, right? In the North Pole we knock on people's doors if we want to talk to them, but a lot of the time people just walk right in if they want to visit. Everyone just loves everyone most of the time in the North Pole but I do know that's not the case here. But I can still knock on her door if we're not friends, right? How else can we become friends if I don't? Do I even want to be her friend? Does she want to be mine? What if she doesn't want to be my friend?

Oh my god, Nik, just knock on the door.

Her brother, Brett, opens the door and tilts his head to the side a little when he sees me.

"Hi," I say with a jolly smile.

"Hi," he says back. But he says it like he's judging me. Shit. I shouldn't have knocked on the door. "You're really into the Santa stuff, eh?"

"What?"

"Your pyjamas. That you're still wearing at 4:30PM. They look like they came from The North Pole."

I look down at my Rudolph slippers and candy cane lounge pants, and then back up at him.

"I was having a lazy day," I defend myself. "And Santa doesn't wear candy cane PJ pants." Except that's a lie, because I'm Santa, and I'm currently wearing candy cane PJ pants.

"I guess you're right. But he can't wear that red suit all the time, right?"

"Why can't I just like candy canes?" I ask. "Or Christmas but not necessarily Santa Claus?"

He smiles and lets out a breath. "I misspoke. I should have said you're really into Christmas stuff."

"That would be correct," I nod. "I do like Christmas stuff. But I think I'm a little behind on some of the traditions and your sister said that she could help me with some stuff yesterday."

"You met Morgan?"

"Yeah. Yesterday."

"Cool. She's not here, sorry."

"Oh. Do you know when she will be here?"

"Tomorrow."

"Shoot. Can uh," I pause, afraid to continue my question. I'm suddenly incredibly nervous and I can feel my fingers shaking. I don't want him to think I'm a loser and decide that I'm not cool enough to be friends with. "Can I," I pause again, thinking I started the question wrong. "I mean…" What's wrong with me?

"Are you okay?" Brett asks.

"I'm sorry, I'm not very good at this, it seems. I've had the same best friend for longer than I can remember, and I don't know how to make new ones."

The corner of his mouth curls into a smile. "You want to come in for a cup of coffee?"

"Oh." I feel my eyebrows raise in surprise. Does Brett want to be my friend? "That would be lovely."

I sit on Brett's couch and he hands me a warm cup of coffee. I hold it in both my hands and wrap my fingers around it so the heat can spread through me.

"So where did you move from?" Brett asks, sitting on the couch across from me. He's got a gentle smile and he looks genuinely interested in my answer. He wants a projector for his bedroom for Christmas.

"Up North," I say.

"Like Sudbury?"

"Oh, much farther North than Sudbury. Um, like the North Pole, basically."

"Ah. So that's why you're so into… um," he looks me up and down. "All this."

I shrug. "Sure. But I actually wanted Morgan to help me with a little Christmas problem."

"What kind of problem?"

"Do you know about Gingerbread Elves?" I ask.

"Of course I do."

"Gingerbread Elf!?" a little voice says. I turn my neck to see little Olivia thumping down the hallway towards us. Her hair is dark like Brett's and Morgan's, but it looks a little tangled in the back. "I have an elf!"

"Oh yeah?" I ask her. "Does your elf move?"

"Yeah! She moves every night when I'm sleeping, but when I wake up, she can't move! So she gets stuck doing the things she was doing at night! She's so silly!"

"Oh. That's so interesting. What do you do to make her move?"

"Nothing!"

"Nothing?" I ask.

"We named her and that gave her Gingerbread Magic and now she can fly!"

"She can fly?"

"Yeah!" And then Olivia puts her arms out as if they're wings and runs back down the hall.

I guess that solves the balls as feet problem. Doesn't explain it, but solves it nonetheless. I turn back to Brett. "I got one yesterday and it hasn't moved. Did I do something wrong?"

"Excuse me?"

"It's still on my kitchen table, even though I gave it a name. I wrote it on the certificate. Am I supposed to frame it or something?"

Brett gives me a bit of an angry glare and makes a cut-it-out motion with his hand, and then whispers quite violently at me, "Olivia might hear you."

"Is that bad?"

"Yes!"

I'm so confused. Brett gets off his couch and moves to sit next to me.

"The fucking doll doesn't move on its own," he whispers.

"Right," I say slowly, feeling like I shouldn't be confused.

"You're supposed to move it when your kid is asleep and when they wake up, they think the elf moved on its own."

"That makes a lot more sense," I say with a bit of a laugh. "But why?"

"What do you mean why?"

I make sure to be as quiet as Brett when I answer. "Why would you make your child believe that a doll is magic and moving around, and talking to Santa about them when they're not?"

"Because it's fun for them."

"But I don't understand."

"What don't you understand?"

"I don't understand why people would make this stuff up?"

"Because it's fun. It's magical. Didn't you think Christmas was magical when you were a kid?"

I wish I could say yes. But I've never experienced Christmas in the way that everyone else has because I'm on the other side of it, and Christmas didn't even exist when I was a kid. I guess it does feel magical, because I literally use magic, and it's always brightened something inside of me when I deliver presents, but I feel like it's a different kind of magic than what Brett is describing. Especially since time slows down now and I haven't been able to witness the children's excitement since before real magic even became involved. But it's quiet. Comforting. Familiar. I don't think it feels the same as it does for everyone else, and in this moment, I'm a little sad about it.

"Yeah," I finally say. "Yeah, it was. I think it was just different for me. We didn't really do any of this stuff when I was growing up."

"Fair enough."

I nod and get up from the couch. "Thanks for the coffee, but I should head out."

"Oh sure, of course. You got big plans for the weekend?"

Oh is it the weekend? I should probably pay attention to these sorts of things.

"Yeah," I say, trying to come up with a believable excuse to leave. "Yeah, I'm going Christmas shopping."

"Good for you. I'm always scrambling to get my Christmas shopping done on the 23rd."

"Of December?" I ask, horrified.

"Yeah," Brett says with a laugh.

"That's much too stressful."

"A little. You'd think I'd learn one of these years, but I never do."

I stare at him, unsure what to say.

"Anyway," Brett says.

"Yes. Right. I should go." I head to the front door of his apartment and he opens it for me. I nod and smile and then step across the hall to my own apartment. I let out a deep breath once I close the door behind me, and lean my head back. I think I just made a friend.

It's late Saturday morning and I hear commotion across the hall. There are thumps and footsteps, but the loudest of everything is roaring laughter. There's a little, higher pitched laugh, as if it's coming from a child, and a bit of a fuller laugh, from an adult. An adult woman, probably. Both laughs are loud, but hearing them makes me happy. I love hearing others' joy. I decide to look through the peep hole to see who it is. Sure enough, it's Olivia and Morgan, and Morgan is almost falling over with laughter as she tries to get the key in the door. Olivia is shoving her, and Morgan shoves her back with her elbow as they continue to laugh. I feel myself smiling as I watch them, so I decide to open the door and ask if they need help. Or maybe I can ask what's so funny? Shoot, I don't know what I should say. Is it strange for me to say anything at all?

Turns out I don't really need to open with something to say, because as soon as I open the door, they both stop and turn to look at me. You can tell they're still in a silly mood though, because they can't keep the grins off their faces and even after they've abruptly stopped, Olivia keeps laughing a little and noticeably tries to stop it before it comes out too much. I smile at them and Morgan says, "Hey! Nik, right?"

I nod my head. "Yeah. Nik. And you're Morgan."

"And I'm Olivia!" Olivia shouts. "My aunty Morgan can't get the door open."

"Shh, we don't have to tell everyone how incompetent I am." Morgan shoves her playfully and winks at me.

"What's incompetent?" Olivia asks.

"It means you're not good at something," Morgan tells her.

"Oh. Cool."

"But your aunt's good at some things, right?" I ask.

"No." Olivia shakes her head and laughs.

"Oh you're so lovely," Morgan says. She puts her key in the door and it seems to go in smoothly from where I'm standing across the hall. She turns it and opens the door without taking the key out. "What are you up to?" she asks.

"Hmm?" I raise my eyebrows at her.

"Are you off somewhere?"

Olivia ducks under Morgan's arm and runs into the apartment.

"Ah, Olivia, what did we say about wet boots!?" she calls after her.

Olivia comes back to the doorway with a pout on her face and this time Morgan lifts her arm so Olivia doesn't have to duck under it to get into the hallway. I watch as both Olivia and Morgan take their boots off and it makes me look down at my own socked feet, and the puddles of brown and grey water all over the floor. They pick their boots up and head inside the apartment before Morgan smiles at me and says, "See ya later," and shuts the door.

Hmm. I guess she didn't really want to know what I was up to.

There's a knock on my door a few hours later so I pause my Christmas movie and get up from the couch to see who it is. Maybe I have mail or something.

But when I open the door, I don't see a mail person, instead I see Morgan with a horrified look on her face. She's got on a black toque with a fluffy pom-pom on top, and her braids come out from underneath it, behind her ears and over both shoulders, sitting nicely on her winter jacket.

"Is something wrong?" I ask.

"What? No. Sorry. I'm just nervous."

"You're nervous? What for?"

"Well I just realized that I'm always sort of running away from you whenever we meet, and I thought it would be nice if we went out for a cup of coffee or something? But I literally never do this so I'm all flustered."

"You never do what?"

"Ask people out."

"Oh. I don't ask people out, either."

"No?" She sounds surprised.

"Never. I've never asked anyone out."

"Really?"

I laugh a little. "Really."

"Oh."

It's quiet for more than a few seconds, so I say, "You have, though."

"Not really."

"Didn't you just ask me out?"

"Oh. Yes. And I mean, I guess I've asked people out before, but not really. Like it was different. I was younger and in college and drunk and stuff."

I narrow my eyes at her. "Of course."

"Anyway. Do you want to get a cup of coffee?"

"That sounds lovely."

She smiles and her horrified look from earlier completely melts away. "There's a nice place down by the water, actually."

"Excellent. The water isn't far, is it? Should we walk?"

"Yeah, that sounds like a nice idea."

The sky is starting to darken and oversized snow flakes float through the air, falling softly and slowly. I watch our footprints on the sidewalk, and mine are quite a bit bigger than hers. But they're almost side by side, each stride the same size. I nudge her mitten with my bare hand and she quickly pulls it into her side.

"Am I walking too fast?" I ask.

"What? No."

"Okay."

"Sorry for pulling my hand away."

I look down at her. "I'm sorry?"

"I thought you were trying to hold my hand and I didn't know what to do."

"Oh, that. I didn't think anything of that. I wasn't trying to hold your hand; I was just getting your attention. But I was actually wondering if I could ask you something."

"Sure."

"What did you mean when you told me to let you know if I needed ideas for The Gingerbread Elf?"

"Like if you didn't know what to do with it."

"I still don't know what you mean. Do what with it?"

"Like putting it in different positions. I do a lot of Olivia's for Brett because he doesn't have a creative bone in his body. He loves seeing her reaction to it though; it's really sweet."

I stop walking and put my hands in my coat pockets. Morgan stops too, and turns to face me.

"I'm going to admit something to you, Morgan. I would appreciate it if you didn't make fun of me or tell others about it."

She smiles. "Okay."

"I don't know what a Gingerbread Elf is."

"Don't you have one?"

"Yes."

"Did you read the book?"

"Yes."

"Then you know what The Gingerbread Elf is."

"That's the thing. I read the book, and I took the doll out of the box, and I wrote its name on its little certificate thing, but I still don't understand it."

"There's nothing to understand, really. It's just another way to make Christmas magical for your kids while also hopefully helping them behave better at the same time."

"Are children embarrassed for the elf to see them behave badly?" I ask.

"No, they won't get presents if they're not good."

I'm shocked. "What? Why not?"

Morgan narrows her eyes at me. "Did you live under a rock before moving here?"

"What?"

"Santa puts coal in your stocking instead of presents if you're not good."

"He does not."

"Well, yeah okay, I know he doesn't *actually*, it's just a scare tactic, but that's how it's always been."

"No," I say confidently. "That must be a newer thing."

"Well I don't know when it started," she says with a laugh.

But I need to know more. "Why do parents have to do things to make Christmas magical?"

She smirks. "Because then Christmas wouldn't be magical." She almost says it like a question, as if I should have known the answer already.

I sigh and start walking again. I don't want to continue and make myself look like I'm delusional, like Charlie had mentioned people might think. But I'm not going to be able to figure out how to get people to believe in me if I don't understand their thought process.

I decide to try a different approach. "Do you have any traditions for Christmas?"

"Well." She takes a deep breath and catches up with me. "When I was growing up, we used to order Chinese food on Christmas Eve and eat it around the coffee table while we watched

A Christmas Story. And on Christmas morning it was always just me, my parents, and my brother. My brother and I were allowed to open our stockings before our parents got up, but we had to wait until they were awake to unwrap anything."

"Your stockings were from Santa?" I ask.

"Of course. And he never wrapped our presents so we would know which ones were from him. But now I just know it was because my parents didn't want to buy different wrapping paper." She laughs, and I want to ask her more about that, but she continues talking before I get a chance. "We would stay in our pyjamas all day and play with our toys and watch Christmas movies, and my mom and dad would make a huge turkey dinner with gravy, and stuffing, and mashed potatoes, and brussel sprouts, and green beans. It was always way too much food for the four of us, but then we got to have turkey sandwiches and turkey soup for the next week. And we always went to my Grandparents' on Boxing Day. My dad's side of the family would all go, and it would be the same kind of dinner that my parents made the night before, only this time there would be more of us and my parents wouldn't have to do anything."

"That sounds so nice," I say.

"Yeah. It was."

"You don't do that anymore, though?"

She shrugs. "No. My brother got married and had Olivia, and they always wanted Christmas to themselves the way we always did, and I had a couple boyfriends over the years, so sometimes I would spend it with their family, and sometimes they would come to my parents' with me. I haven't really done the same thing for Christmas since before Olivia was born."

"And how old is Olivia?" I ask.

"She's seven."

"Is Brett not with his wife anymore? I haven't seen her."

Morgan stops walking. "Ah." I stop walking as well and watch her. Her face falls a little and then she looks up at me. "Brett's wife died two years ago."

"Oh. I'm sorry."

"Yeah. It sucked. It still sucks. It was a car accident so it was really sudden. Obviously." She shakes her head quickly and then keeps walking. "I actually got The Gingerbread Elf for Olivia their first Christmas without her, and I think it helped them both. I moved the Elf most nights, and Brett and Olivia would look for her together every morning to see what kind of trouble she had gotten into. Brett and I moved her together sometimes, and he did it on his own a few times as well. I think Brett felt the magic the most when he moved the Elf himself, even though when you think about it, it's the least magical because you're ruining the magic by seeing it all be done, by doing it yourself. Right? Like showing someone how to do a magic trick, only you're the only one who's in on it. But it's actually not. It's more magical because you're the one making it, you know? You're literally making magic for your child, and it's so cool."

"That actually does sound really cool," I say, but I'm still confused and I have no idea how to get her to tell me *why* everyone is making things up but telling their kids that they aren't. Why aren't they just letting me do my job?

We've made it to the coffee shop, which has white twinkle lights around the outside of the windows. They glow through a soft layer of snow and it's so pretty and calming that I want to stand and look at them forever.

"You okay?" Morgan asks me.

"Yeah," I say. "The lights are just really nice coming through the snow."

"Oh. Yeah, they are. I love Christmas lights."

"Me too."

"I like the colourful ones better though." She smiles and scrunches her nose at me before opening the door and motioning for me to go inside.

"So do I," I say, stepping into the warm building. My nose and cheeks feel the difference in temperature immediately and I love the feeling of them still being cold as the warmth surrounds me. There are twinkle lights hanging from the wooden beams in the ceiling, and I decide that I love it in here.

"What kind of coffee do you like?" she asks me, stepping closer to the counter.

"Anything sweet, I guess."

"You like sweet coffees? That's amazing."

"It is?"

"Yeah. Most guys are too insecure to even try a sweet coffee, or god forbid an alcoholic drink that's colourful."

"That's the silliest thing I've ever heard." Except that it isn't. Gingerbread Elves travelling to the North Pole every night is probably the silliest thing I've ever heard.

"I'm glad you think so. I'm getting a Christmas Cookie Latte. Do you want one?"

"That sounds delightful," I say with a little shrug.

"Excellent."

She orders two Christmas Cookie Lattes and the man behind the counter makes them with a smile. She taps her card on the machine and waves my hand away when I try to tap my own card.

"I invited you out," she says.

"So?"

"So the invitee shouldn't have to pay."

I sigh, but give her a smile. "You're right. Thank you."

"Of course."

The person behind the counter puts two green mugs with whipped cream and sprinkles coming out of the top on the counter for us, and Morgan picks up both of them and leads me to a couch beside a fire place.

"It's really nice in here," I say.

She hands me my mug and I smile as I take it. "Yeah, I love it here," she says.

"I can see why."

I take a sip of my latte but I mostly just get a mouthful of whipped cream. I try again and this time a bit of the warm drink comes through. It's sweet and delicious, and I love the contrast of temperatures between it and the cold whipped cream in my mouth at the same time.

"Mmm," I hum. "This is really good."

"I'm glad you like it. It's my favourite. I wish they had it all year round, though."

"Yeah, that would be nice. I have another question about the Gingerbread Elf, though."

Morgan chuckles and nods her head. "Sure."

"Why don't they have feet?"

"They have feet!"

"No," I say, shaking my head almost violently. "They have balls."

"They're gumballs! I thought you said you read the book!"

"Uh, I did?"

"Bouncing around on gumball feet?"

"I don't know what that means," I say.

She laughs again. "It's from the book.

> *From the North Pole in Gingerbread Gear*
> *But you're fast asleep so you can't hear*
> *You just wait, you're in for a treat*
> *Your Elf is bouncing around on gumball feet.*"

"I'm not sure I understand," I say slowly.

"They have gumballs for feet. They bounce on them."

"Olivia said they fly."

"Yes, they fly from the North Pole, but apparently when they're inside, they bounce."

"On gumballs."

"Yes." She smiles and sits up a little straighter like she's proud. "Again, I thought you said you read the book."

"I read the book, but I was already confused and frustrated about-" I cut myself off when I realize I was about to reveal too much, and try again. "Uh, about something personal, and I guess I just didn't catch that it was being literal. Gumballs aren't bouncy, for one."

"No, but magical gumballs are."

"Magical Gingerbread Magic Gumballs," I say.

"There you go, now you're getting it," she laughs.

I smirk and tilt my head a little, letting myself feel comfortable joking around with her.

"So what do you usually do for Christmas?" she asks, sinking into the cushion behind her and leaning her head back a little, angling it to the side to look at me.

What a question. How am I supposed to answer that? I don't really know what other people do for Christmas so I don't even know how to make anything up. But I want to make something up. I suddenly want to make something up so badly and I want her to think it's amazing. I want her to smile up at me with a twinkle in her eye and give a sigh of comfort at my story. I want her to like me. I don't really know what this feeling is, but it's making my chest all warm and fuzzy. What do I do? What do I say? Is this normal?

"I'm going to be as honest as I can," I say slowly. It's weird feeling like your entire existence needs to be a secret. Everyone talks about Santa and I can't tell anyone he's me.

She twists her head a little as if she's taken aback. "Okay."

"I'm not sure I can tell you my Christmas tradition. It's really different from everyone else's and I'm afraid of what you would think of me if I told you. I don't even know you, and I want you to like me."

"Okay," she says again, but slowly this time. "Well like, can you give me a hint? Because if I wouldn't like you because of it, maybe there's a reason?"

"I don't know how to explain it. I just moved from very far North, and I lived in a very isolated part of the world. I knew everyone in my town and they were more than neighbours to me, they were family. I feel like the world works very differently down here."

"Hmm," she says, clearly thinking. "I know communities can have a different feel to them depending on where they are or how many people live there, but I don't think they really do anything different enough to mean I wouldn't like you. Unless you were in a cult or something?"

I laugh and rub my hand on my thigh. I think I'm nervous.

"Does that mean you were in a cult?" she asks.

"No. No, I wasn't in a cult. I just." I let out a breath and then take a sip of my latte. It really is very good. I lean forward and put my mug down on the coffee table and then bend my knee and bring my leg up onto the couch so I can face Morgan better. "I... I delivered everyone presents."

"In your town?"

"Yes," I say as confidently as I can.

"So you played Santa? Did you dress up as him?"

"Yeah, I guess I did."

"That's so cute. Did everyone know it was you?"

"Yes, everyone knew it was me. There was a bit of a tradition every year where all the elve-" I cut myself off and try to recover as naturally as possible but I'm not sure I do a good job. "All the people in town would see me off. They would gather in the town square, which was actually more of a circle, and we would all count down together the last ten seconds before I took off. Um, on foot. I would walk. It was a small town."

"How did you have the money to buy everyone in town in a present? And what started it all? You just said that you wanted to do it one year and everyone agreed?"

"It started slowly," I say. "Sort of by accident. At first, I just did it secretly for a few families who couldn't afford it. But it made them so happy, even people who didn't get presents were happy and excited about it, so I kept going. I added more families each year, and eventually people found out that it was me doing it, and they all wanted to help, so people started building toy-" I cut myself off again and clear my throat. "People started pitching in with money to buy presents. Some people bought presents and donated them to the cause. But they all wanted me to deliver them still, and they didn't want any credit."

"That's literally the sweetest thing I've ever heard. You were like your town's own real Santa Claus."

I smile. "Yeah."

"What are they going to do without you?"

"Maybe someone will take over." Maybe Susan. "Um, but when you say real Santa Claus," I continue. But I don't finish because I don't really know how to. I know what I want to say, but I guess I'm afraid to say it.

"Yes?" she asks.

"Well, what do you mean?"

"What do I mean by real Santa Claus?"

"Yeah."

"It's pretty self explanatory, don't you think?"

"Yes," I say slowly. "Very self explanatory."

"Why would you think that story would make me not like you?" she asks, getting away from my question.

"Oh, I don't know. I thought maybe you would think that I was weird. Or that I thought I was Santa, or something."

She laughs and throws her head back a little. I laugh too, but only so she's not the only one. When she calms down a bit she leans forward and giggles quietly, putting her hand on my arm. I look down at her fingers gently laying across my jacket and then I look back up at her.

"Sorry," she says, pulling her hand back.

"Oh. It's quite alright."

"Anyway, we can talk about something other than Christmas."

And we do. We talk until the café closes, and she tells me about her brother and his wife who passed away. Her name was Ashley, and Ashley and her were good friends. She said that even if Brett didn't need help with Olivia during his grieving, she would have done it anyway because it helped her to grieve in her own way. The three of them sort of got their own new routine going during the first year that Ashley was gone, and even though Brett feels better doing most things on his own now, they still keep their routine. It feels stable, sort of safe. And she knows that Olivia takes comfort in it, so she continues to take her to school most days, and stays for supper throughout the week. Brett and Morgan make dinner together a few nights a week, and it's been a great way for them to keep their relationship close.

We walk across town to a beer brewery called The Friendly Taproom so that we can continue our conversation, and honestly

I'm glad she suggested it, because I didn't want our evening to end so soon. And what a perfect name for this place, because as soon as I walk in I can feel the warmth radiating throughout the entire space. It feels welcoming just like the coffee shop did, and I immediately feel relaxed as I look around at the couches set up like living rooms, and at families and friends sharing large tables. Everyone behind the bar seems to be having a good time as they talk to the patrons, and already I feel like I belong. Morgan pulls herself onto a bar-style stool at a tall table near the bar, and puts her coat across the small back of the chair. I do the same with my coat and sit across from her, resting my feet on the cross bar of my stool.

"They're always making new beer here," she says, picking up a menu. "So there's almost always something new to try when you come in."

"Oh that sounds like fun," I say.

"You feel like eating anything?" she asks me, picking up a menu from the table in front of her.

"Sure." I pick up my own menu and look through the options. Everything sounds so delicious, but I settle on a tomato soup and grilled cheese. Something warm and cozy seems like the perfect option for a snowy evening.

Morgan gets the same thing, and we each get something called a beer flight so we can try different ones and compare the flavours. I'd never heard of this concept before and I'm delighted when Morgan explains it to me. The beer samples come in cute little glasses and they all sit in a wooden plank of sorts, with a label across the front so you know which one you're drinking. We carry them back to our table from the bar and share our thoughts as we try them and wait for our food to come out.

Morgan doesn't like two of hers, but I do, so I drink them for her with a smile. My head starts to feel a little fuzzy before I'm done all my soup, and I realize that I'm getting drunk. I haven't been drunk in about five hundred years, so I'm afraid that I'm going to make a fool of myself.

"Oh dear," I say quietly.

"What?" Morgan asks. "What's wrong?"

"I do believe I'm drunk."

She giggles and takes a sip of beer. "You haven't even had two pints worth."

"Yeah, it doesn't take much when you don't drink."

"You don't drink?"

I shake my head. "Well, not on purpose. No, that doesn't make sense. I just don't, I don't know. I like hot chocolate and cookies better."

"Well, how drunk are you?"

"Not very. Just more than I have been in a very long time."

She smirks. "Okay. Well that's fine. Just don't act too drunk so we don't get cut off."

"Cut off?"

"Yeah. Told we can't drink anymore."

"Oh, I definitely shouldn't drink anymore."

"Okay. Well, I want a glass of this sour one, it's really good." She gets up from the table and makes her way to the bar to order her drink. She comes back with two glasses, one with her beer and the other with what looks like ice water. She puts the glass of water on the table in front of me and smiles as she climbs back into her seat.

"I'm having a lot of fun," I say.

"So am I. Thanks for hanging out with me."

"Of course. Actually, I have a question for you."

"Shoot."

"Do you have an Apple Pencil?" I ask.

"Yes, why?"

"I've never used one."

"No?"

I shake my head. "Is that weird?"

Morgan shrugs and laughs a little. "No, why would that be weird? I mean, they're mostly only popular with artists."

"Are you an artist?"

It looks like she hesitates for a second, looks away towards the bar, and then back to me. "I dabble," she says.

"Oh? Are you learning?"

She shrugs and smiles a little. "Uh, not really. Why are you so interested?"

"I just haven't used one before. Or an iPad, even. I've seen them a lot, in their packages. And Apple Pencils I've seen, out of their packages, but that's it."

Morgan scrunches her face a little, as if she's confused or concerned. "That doesn't make a lot of sense. Maybe you should have some of that water, lushy."

"I don't know what that means." I take a big gulp of the ice water and it's so delicious and makes my insides cold as it goes down.

"Well if you want, you can try mine out."

"Right now?"

"Oh. Um. No, my iPad's at my place. But maybe another time. I'll bring it to my brother's the next time I'm there."

"That sounds amazing!"

Morgan laughs and takes a sip of her beer.

"Why is that funny?" I ask.

"It's not really, I just love how excited you are."

"Oh. Okay."

She smiles at me but doesn't say anything else. I'm not sure what to say to continue the conversation, but I do enjoy looking at her. She's very pretty. Her braids sort of frame her round cheeks, and her smile is so easy that it makes me want to smile more myself. Something about being in her presence makes me feel cozy. I notice that she's just been looking at me too, and I wonder if she's thinking the same thing about me.

"You know a lot of really great spots," I finally say to break the silence.

"Oh. Yeah. The town just has a lot of them. A lot of really great people who opened their own businesses and treat their staff well. Next, I can take you to my favourite pizza place. It's not fast food pizza, it's sort of fancy."

"I've never had fancy pizza before."

"Okay, then I'm definitely taking you," she says with a grin that shows her teeth.

I feel my smile grow. "Okay."

MORGAN

Ohmygod this man is so hot. I can't stop staring at him, and to be honest, I would be content just sitting here staring at him until after the Brewery closes. His hair is short but thick, and looks like it wants me to run my fingers through it. And his salt and pepper beard? Yum. It's hard to tell because he's always wearing cozy looking hoodies, but it doesn't seem like he works out or anything, so he's probably soft and squishy. Even if he isn't, I just want to climb inside of him.

Oh god. That's a strange thing to say. I take a few big gulps of my beer to try and calm myself of this intense reaction over a man I don't even know, but immediately regret it. I forgot how sour this beer was, and I pucker before I'm done swallowing my third gulp. I close my eyes and try to stop my face from getting all twisted but I can't help it.

Nik laughs and I giggle a little in return. "Pro tip," I start, trying to swallow all the extra saliva in my mouth before continuing so I don't spit all over the table, "don't gulp a sour beer if you want to remain chill."

"Hey, I'm not against people losing their chill."

"Wow, we both sound so old," I laugh.

"We do?"

"Yeah. We sound like old parents trying to keep up with the times but are failing."

"Oh boy," Nik says with a bit of a grimace.

"It's fine, it happens to everyone at some point."

"Right. Of course."

"Morgan!" I hear someone call. I turn towards the bar and spot the owner looking over at us with a huge smile. He waves and comes over to our table.

"Hey Paul," I say to him. Then I turn to Nik. "This is Paul, the owner."

"Oh cool. I'm Nik."

"Nice to meet you," Paul replies.

I watch Nik reach his hand out and shake Paul's. Then they both look at me as if I'm supposed to say something important, but I just smile and let out a breath. I can tell that Paul wants to ask if we're on a date, but I also know that he won't, which I appreciate.

"Nik just moved into my brother's building," I say after a minute of awkward silence.

"Oh, excellent," Paul says. "How do you like Morgan's artwork?"

I snort and almost choke on my beer, at the same time that Nik says, "Morgan's artwork?" but he sort of cuts himself off when he realizes that I'm having difficulty breathing. Some of the beer has come out my nose and I grab a napkin to wipe it away while I cough as discreetly as possible.

"Are you okay?" they both ask. Paul briefly puts a hand on my back and Nik raises himself from his chair and leans over the table towards me.

I nod, but keep coughing, so I'm not sure how convinced they are. Nik actually walks around the table to me and rubs my back, which is the most calming thing I've ever experienced. Oh my god I want to lean into his chest and have him wrap his arms around me and let me breathe in his hoodie and then rip it off. I finally stop coughing and I smile up at him.

"Thanks," I say, and then take a few deep breaths.

"I'm sorry I made you choke," Paul says.

"No, no," I say, waving him off. "I'm fine, just mortified is all." I don't want him to feel like he said anything wrong so I try to lighten the mood with a laugh. I'm afraid there's still beer dripping from my nose so I wipe my face with the napkin again.

"Well I don't want to do any further physical or emotional damage so, uh, I'll just go back to the bar now." He blushes and shakes his head as he walks away. I hope he doesn't feel too bad.

"Are you alright?" Nik asks. "What happened?"

"He just caught me off guard," I say with a shrug.

"When he asked if I liked your artwork?"

"Yeah," I say a little quietly.

"So you *are* an artist?" he asks, like he's completely interested.

"No," I stammer, and I have no idea why. I don't mean to lie, I just didn't want to tell him about my art right off the bat. "I mean yeah," I say, and then close my eyes. I don't know how to tell him that I always feel weird telling people about my art, especially before I really know them. I just feel like I'm bragging, or like I'm just fishing for compliments. That sounds so silly, sillier than lying about being an artist, which I sort of already started doing, so instead of giving him an explanation, I just stare at him, horrified.

"Do you want to show me any of it, so I can answer him, or is it private?" He asks the question with such a kind tone that I now feel terrible for lying to him. I didn't mean to lie to him per se, I just wasn't planning on telling him about my art just yet, and I didn't know he was going to ask me about Apple Pencils.

I continue to stare at him, unsure how to recover. He's looking at me like he's interested, like he really wants to know, but not because he's nosy, because he wants to understand. It just feels like he wants to be a part of things with me. I've never gotten this feeling from someone before, especially not from just a look, like he's currently giving me, so I don't know if anyone can say they've experienced the same thing. But there you have it.

I sigh and say, "It's not private, it's all over the beer cans."

"What?" Nik walks over to the take-out fridges and I only just realize that his hand was still on my back that whole time. I feel lost all of a sudden without his gentle touch. He grabs two colourful cans and brings them back to the table, setting them next to his glass of water. "You did this?"

"Yeah," I say.

"This is amazing! If I did this, I would be telling everyone."

"Yeah, that's what everyone says."

"So why aren't you telling everyone?"

I shrug as I take the last drink of beer from my glass. "I feel weird about it."

"Why?"

"I don't know. I just don't like bragging."

"It's not bragging. But even if it was, you deserve to brag. This is incredible."

"Thank you," I say. I can feel my face heating up.

"Is that what you do for a living? Do the artwork for the beer here?"

"And for other businesses. I also have. Um. A gallery."

"What? You have a gallery? You told me ten minutes ago that you 'dabbled' in art, but you have a *gallery?*"

"Yeah," I say with half my voice. "It's really small. But it's a nice space for me to do my work with less distractions, and I'll sell the occasional print. And I sold an original once."

"Can I see it?" he asks. "Your gallery?"

"Really? You want to see my gallery?"

"Hell yes. Why wouldn't I want to?"

"I don't know. Because we just met?"

"So?"

"Okay. Um." I grab my coat from the back of my chair and start to put it on. "Do you want to go now?"

"Yeah! I'm going to buy these beers first, though."

We walk together in the crisp night air towards my gallery, which is just around the corner. All the shops downtown are closed by now, the only people on the streets probably coming or going from restaurants. I pull my keys out of my bag and stop in front of the door where Nik gasps.

"You have a sign and everything! And hours on the glass door in little white letters!"

I chuckle. "I do."

"This is so cool."

I unlock the door and step inside the dark gallery, feeling on the wall for the light switch. I flick it on and all my paintings on the wall are lit up with perfectly placed lighting. I have canvases and frames holding paintings of deer in the snow, of fae girls reaching for frogs on lily pads, of happy dogs in the sun. Baby ducks with flower hats.

"These are amazing," Nik says, walking towards a painting of a mouse holding a sword up in triumph. "How much is this one? Oh never mind, I see the price here. Can I buy it now or should we wait until you're open?"

"You- you want to buy the warrior mouse?"

"Yes. Looking at it makes me feel cozy."

"Really?"

"Really. Anyway, can I buy it?"

"Y-yes," I stammer. "Of course you can buy it. Are you sure you don't just want a print of it, though? It's much cheaper."

"No, I want the original."

"Sure. Yeah. Um. Yes, you can buy it." I pull my phone out and open the Square app and then grab the card reader from behind the counter. "Do you have a card?" I ask.

"Yes." He pulls his wallet from his back pocket and puts his card in the reader. I hand my phone to him so he can put his PIN in, and I watch as he taps the screen with his index finger, and then I look away, realizing I'm totally watching him put in his PIN. He hands my phone back and I take it with a smile.

"I can leave it here for you until it isn't snowing," I say. "I can still wrap it up, but if you don't want to risk it getting wet-"

"Yeah, sure, that would be nice."

"I can bring it to you, actually. If you want."

"Sounds great."

"Cool."

"So you lied to me about being an artist because you," he pauses, raising an eyebrow, "felt weird about it?"

"I didn't lie. Technically."

"I asked you if you were an artist and you said you dabbled."

"Yeah? So?"

"And then I asked if you were learning and you said no."

"Yeah, because I'm not learning," I say with a hint of a smirk. "Technically."

"Technically," he repeats, a playful tone in his voice.

"Anyway, I'm sorry," I say.

"Don't be sorry. I just don't understand why anyone would want to hide such joy from anyone."

I almost gasp at him calling my artwork 'joy', but all I can do is look up at him. No one has ever acted this way about my art before. Of course my family and friends are excited for me, and past supportive boyfriends have been too, but sometimes it feels like they're just excited because they know me, or because they feel like they have to be. I've done well doing art for local businesses, but no one ever really seems interested in my originals. Plus no guy I've dated recently has ever been excited like Nik to look at my art, or said that my paintings make them feel cozy. They've chuckled and called them cute, which to be fair, a lot of them absolutely are, but the tone they always used didn't make it feel like a compliment. A few guys have been excited that I do the artwork for the beer, but, like, in a weird way? One guy actually said to me once, 'I can't believe a girl does such cool artwork for beer'. Like. Thanks? What does being a *woman* have anything to do with it?

"Thanks," I say. "I'll try not to hide it from people from now on."

"You can hide things from people if you want to. I was just saying that I don't understand wanting to."

"I don't *really* want to hide it," I try. "I just wish I was more confident."

"So do I." I smile at him but he continues talking. "Having your own gallery is pretty confident, though. Is it weird to say that I'm proud of you?"

"I guess it's not weird," I say slowly.

"I know we don't really know each other, but I am. I'm so proud of you for doing all of this and for opening your own gallery even though you don't feel confident."

"Thanks," I say.

I step a little closer to him as if there's some outside force pulling me to him. What is it about him that just makes me want to curl up on the couch with him? He radiates joy, more than my artwork apparently does, and he's so gorgeous, and he always looks so cozy, like it's his job, or like he grew up in a teddy bear factory or something. I take another step towards him. He watches me as I get closer and I can't tell if he wants me to or not. I want to unzip his jacket and slide my hands inside, I want to grab onto the kangaroo pocket of his hoodie and pull him into me. Instead I just step into him more and look into his dark brown eyes.

"Hi," I whisper.

"Hi." He smiles down at me and then reaches his hands out to mine. I let him link our fingers together and I look down at them briefly before finding his gaze again.

"I never do this," I say.

"Never do what?"

"Get this close to someone I just met."

"Oh," he says. "Me neither."

"Really?"

"Yes."

I push onto my toes and press my lips to his. He kisses me back, and I pull my hands from his so that I can wrap my arms around his neck. He opens his mouth to mine and I run my fingers through his hair, wishing he would do more than rest his hands on my waist. I push myself into him and then grab at the zipper of his coat, pulling it down and opening it all the way. He doesn't move to unzip mine, so I do it myself and let my coat fall to the floor. I run my hands up to his shoulders and try to get him to shrug it off but he puts his hands on mine and slows down our kiss.

"Hey," he says, not really taking his mouth from mine. "I'm not…" he kisses me again and then wraps his arms around me. "I'm not really sure…" he kisses me one more time and then pulls back a little. "I'm not really sure how I feel about this," he finally says.

I step back and throw my hands to my mouth. "Oh my god. Oh my god, I'm so sorry."

"No, no, it's okay."

"No it isn't. Oh my god. Oh my *god*, I just threw myself at you like you were a consenting human and I didn't even ask."

"I am a consenting human," he says quietly.

"No you're not. You just said you're not sure how you feel about it! Oh my god, I'm a terrible person."

"I wanted you to kiss me," he says, putting a hand out to me. "I wanted to kiss you, but I was afraid to kiss you, so I was hoping you would do it. I'm glad you did. I just also feel unsure."

"If I asked you if I could kiss you, would you have said yes, or would you have said you weren't sure?"

"I would have said yes."

"What are you unsure about?" I ask.

He shrugs a little. "I haven't done anything like this in a really long time and I just feel a little out of my element, I suppose."

"Okay. I'm still sorry. I was just reading into everything wrong, I guess. The whole time that we've hung out tonight, I've felt incredibly cozy with you, and I thought-- I don't know, I guess I didn't think you felt the same, but I hoped you did. But you just feel so safe, you know? That's a weird thing to say."

"No, it isn't weird. I get that a lot, actually."

"You do? From all the women you haven't done this with?"

He smirks a little. "No, from everyone. People always seem drawn to me and feel like they already know me. That could be why you got close to me even though you don't normally get close to men you've just met."

"I guess."

"Which is another reason why I'm unsure."

"Oh?" I ask.

"Yeah." He lets out a deep breath and looks away for a second. "I don't think I can tell you about it. Not yet, anyway."

"Oh?" I ask again.

"Maybe we should go," he half whispers.

"Okay." I nod, feeling embarrassed, and then pick my coat up off the floor. I look away as I put it back on and then I grab my keys from the counter and turn back towards the door where Nik is waiting. "Um," I say. "After you."

He nods and smiles, and opens the door. I follow him out and lock the door behind us. This walk back is going to be hard. I know he said he wanted to kiss me, but I'm still embarrassed for basically jumping him before I knew if he wanted me to. He did grab onto my hands though, which was definitely a sign that he wanted to kiss me. Yes? Ugh.

But I'm delighted when Nik grabs my hand and curls his fingers around mine. I'm even more delighted when he puts both our hands in his fuzzy coat pocket, and even *more* delighted when he rubs the back of my hand with his thumb. I lean into his shoulder and press into his side as we walk. This is probably the coziest I've ever felt in my entire life.

I walk Nik to his apartment since I have to get my car to go home anyway, and we stop in front of his door.

"Thank you for inviting me out," he says.

"Of course. Thanks for coming. And for buying my painting."

"Oh yeah, I'm really excited about the painting. I'm so excited to show it to Charlie."

"Charlie?" I ask.

"Oh. My best friend."

"Oh. That's cute."

"It is?"

I feel myself smiling. "Sure."

"Do you want to come in for some hot chocolate?" he asks.

"That would be nice, actually. But only if you have mini marshmallows."

"Are they really that important?"

"I'm kidding."

"Of course. But I think I have mini marshmallows anyway."

I follow him inside and quietly shut the door behind me. His Christmas tree is set up in the corner of the living room and there's also lights around the windows that he turns on as I hang up my coat. He has a deep sectional with fluffy looking pillows and I sort of just want to flop onto it with all my weight.

I step into the kitchen where he's putting two mugs on the counter, and I catch a glimpse of his Gingerbread Elf on the table behind him.

"So how old is your kid?" I ask, feeling a lump forming in my throat.

"My kid? I don't have a kid."

"Oh, I'm sorry. I thought you had shared custody of a kid or something."

"Why would you think that?"

"You bought a Gingerbread Elf."

"I just bought it because I was curious about it," he says.

"Oh."

"Yeah. No kids for me."

"Good. I mean. Oh, that sounded bad. Having kids isn't good or bad, it's just-"

Thankfully Nik cuts me off and says, "It's okay, I'm not offended either way. I love kids. They're fantastic and full of wonder and joy, and they make me really happy, and I love to make them happy, but I don't think I want any of my own."

Suddenly a weight lifts off me. Not that I want to marry this guy, but a few times I've thought a relationship was going somewhere good with a guy just for me to find out he wants to have kids. I love my niece, and I love helping Brett out with her, but I just don't want one of my own, full time. I don't even want to be pregnant. But I figured if Nik had a kid, that he probably didn't have them full time and maybe that would be okay, especially if they were already Olivia's age or maybe even older. But I'm still relieved at his answer.

"Do you want kids?" Nik asks me.

I shake my head a little and smile. "No. I like being an aunt."

"That's cool. Hot chocolate's ready. How many marshmallows do you want?"

We sit on Nik's couch with our hot chocolate and watch *A Christmas Story*. By the time we're halfway through the movie I've managed to snuggle into his side and he's put his arm around me.

I breathe out a sigh of contentment and let myself ease into him. He's as comfy to cuddle with as I was anticipating, and when I relax deeper into him, I swear I can feel him relaxing too. How can I feel so close to this man so quickly? Is he made of magic?

Something brushes my nose and I open my eyes, only to realize that I'd fallen asleep.

"Sorry," I say, leaning away from him and then sitting up.

"Oh, it's okay. I just wasn't sure if you needed to get home."

"Oh. Yeah, I probably should, eh?"

"Only if you want to."

"I do recall you saying you were unsure about all of this, so whether or not I want to go home, I think I should."

He nods and gives me a weak smile. "You're right. Thank you for not, um," he scratches his beard and laughs a little. "Thanks for not being offended. You're not offended, are you?"

"No, not at all. Is it okay if I use your washroom before I head out?"

"Yes, absolutely."

I go around the couch to the little dining area by the kitchen, and then I glance back to see if he's watching me. He's turning the TV off and straightening the cushions on the couch, so I grab his Elf off the table and quickly hide it in my shirt before darting through the kitchen and down the hall.

I sneak into his bedroom and tiptoe towards his dresser. He's got Old Spice antiperspirant in the corner of the dresser, along with a black comb and a fancy pocket watch. It's made of silver, or a silver-like metal, and I run my fingers along the beautiful etching of an intricate snowflake across the cover. I look back towards the hallway, and I still seem to be alone, so I pull the elf doll out from my shirt and sit him on the dresser, leaning his back against the wall so he doesn't fall over. I pop the watch open and set it next to the doll, and position his arm over the top of the opened cover.

Before I get caught, I tiptoe quickly out of Nik's room and into the bathroom, where I shut the door and force myself to pee.

"I should get your number," I say to Nik as I'm putting my boots on at his door.

"Oh, yes. About that."

I raise my eyebrows at him, but I don't say anything in return.

"I don't have a cell phone," he says.

"What? You don't have a cell phone? How do you do anything?"

"What do you mean how do I do anything? I do many things that you don't need a cell phone for."

"Sorry, I meant like, how do you make plans with friends? Or look things up?"

"I don't look things up, and I don't have any friends."

"What about Charlie?"

"Oh yes, Charlie is my friend. I meant that I don't have any friends here. And back home, Charlie and I didn't need cell phones."

"So what do I do if I want to call you? Or make plans with you?"

"Um…"

All of a sudden my heart shoots into my throat and my fingertips shake a little. "I mean, that is of course, if you want to be my friend." Oh god, my mouth is dry too.

"Of course I want to be your friend."

Oh good. Despite this being a relief to hear, my heart is still pounding and probably will be until after I've made it home. "Okay," I manage to say.

"I'll go to the store tomorrow and get a cell phone," he says.

"Do you want company?"

"I would love company. And help, actually, if you know anything about phones. Because I sure don't."

"Sure, yeah, I'd love to help. You want me to pick you up? Around 11?"

"That sounds great."

"Okay. See you tomorrow, then."

"Yeah. See you tomorrow."

Okay, my insides are no longer plotting against me, and I can't hold back my grin as I walk down the hall towards the stairwell. I practically skip to my car and then I sing loudly to all the songs that come on the radio. I skip across the parking lot to my building and hum while the elevator takes me to my floor. He seems to like me, he just wants to take it slow. I'm okay with slow. Going slow is normally my preference anyway, and the fact that he's the one who brought it up makes me feel even more secure in this friendship and possibly-more-than-that-ship in the future. And if we just stay friends, that's okay too. Friends are great.

I'm not even nervous as I drive over to Nik's the next morning, and I'm confident and happy as I climb the stairs and make my way towards his door. I feel a little bad being here in my brother's building without going to visit him. Maybe I'll stop by before heading back home. I'm about to knock on Nik's door when he opens it. I jump back a little, startled, and then laugh.

"Sorry," he says with a chuckle.

"Oh, it's okay. Are you ready?"

He straightens up a little. "Yes."

He steps into the corridor and together we walk down to my car. I want to ask him about his elf, but I also want him to bring it up. I don't want it to be obvious that I was the one who moved it, even though it's obvious that I'm the one who moved it. But I have to say I'm a little disappointed that he hasn't said anything, even in a playful way, about it.

I decide to give it more time, let it come up more organically, and I drive us uptown, past Laser Tag, and towards the strip mall that has a McDonald's, a Harvey's, a print shop, a few clothing stores, and an electronics store. I notice Nik looking out the window at everything as I drive, and when I park the car, I look over at him.

"You okay?" I ask.

"Oh yes. I just haven't been up this way yet. It's so different from the part of town that's by the water."

"Yes, that's downtown. Most downtowns are like that."

"Where I'm from the whole town is like downtown. Only merrier, and cozy, and always covered in super fluffy snow."

"Merrier, eh? Sounds nice."

"It is."

I smile and undo my seat belt, so Nik does the same, and together we go to find him a phone.

We settle on a lower end smart phone, because when I explain them all to him, he insists that he won't need 'any of that stuff'.

"Do you want to come to my place and try out my Apple Pencil?" I ask him once we're back in the car.

"Oh, can we?" He sounds like a little kid excited to go get ice cream.

I can't get over how excited he is. He's practically bouncing in his seat as I drive to my place, and I try to not laugh because I don't want him to feel self conscious but I can't help but giggle a little.

"I'm afraid you're going to be disappointed," I say, turning onto my street.

"Oh, I don't think I will be."

"Okay," I say. "Except that I think you will. You're overhyping this so much."

"I don't think I am."

I laugh. "Okay."

We pull into the parking lot for my building and Nik's smile grows. He looks at me with a head tilt and I bulge my eyes at him, unsure what he's trying to say.

"What?" I ask.

"You live in a real apartment building," he says with awe in his voice.

"What does that mean?" I laugh. "You live in a real apartment building, too."

"But this one is tall. And has balconies. Like in the movies."

"Okay," I say with a smile. I pull into my parking spot and then look over at Nik. "Ready?"

"Yes!"

"Okay," I say again, laughing.

He grabs my hand once we're both out of the car and I shove my shoulder into his upper arm. He shoves me back and I squeal. I want to kiss him while we wait in the elevator but I also just want to hang out with him and get to know him more. I think kissing him will be a million times better when we know each other better. It's just weird because it already feels like we know each other but I know we don't. I wonder what's making me feel this way, and I wonder if he feels it too.

Watching Nik play with the Apple Pencil is like watching a child on Christmas. He's so thrilled to just be holding it. His smile is so big that his face probably hurts.

"Do you use this to make the art for the beer cans?" he asks me.

"Yes."

"But you use paint for everything else?"

"I use paint for all my own artwork. I use digital art for all my business clients. Like for logos and stuff like that."

"Oh, cool."

"Yeah."

"Tell me again why you didn't want me to know about this?"

"I don't know," I sigh. "I didn't want to tell you I was an artist just yet. And I didn't *not* want to tell you, I just wanted to get a better feel for you first. The last couple guys haven't taken me seriously when I told them about it, and it's really disheartening."

"Really?"

"Yeah," I almost whisper.

"I'm sorry people did that. And I'm sorry if that's part of the reason that you're not as confident as you should be."

"Why are you like this?"

"Like what?"

"Like this! You're so understanding and amazing and always know the right thing to say."

"Oh, I don't know about that." He shrugs a little and taps the Apple Pencil on his left palm a few times, and then looks back down at the iPad.

"It's true. You know I didn't plan on kissing you right away, right?"

"Hmm?" He looks back to me and actually blushes.

"Sorry, I didn't mean to blurt that out. I just wanted you to know."

He smiles. "Okay."

He doesn't say anything else, and I'm not sure why I felt the need to bring that up, so I cross the room to see what he's been drawing, and I chuckle at his cartoon of a snowman.

"That's cute," I say.

"Thanks. But snowmen are pretty easy to draw."

"I guess. Do you want to go for pizza?" I ask.

He looks up at me as if I've caught him off guard, and then back at the iPad. "Oh. Sure."

"We don't have to." Now I'm worried that I'm coming on too strong. Talking about our kiss and *also* asking him out for pizza? After he told me he wasn't sure?

"No, I want to. Let's go." He puts the pencil and iPad down, and smiles as he stands up.

We go to Carter's for pizza and my favourite server, Felix, greets us at the door.

"Hey, Morgan!" Felix says with a smile. "I haven't seen you in forever, how's it going?"

"Good, you? How's Reese? I haven't seen her in a long time."

"We're both good. Is it just the two of you today?"

I look at Nik and then back at Felix. "Yes. This is Nik, by the way."

"Nice to meet you," Nik says.

Felix smiles and nods and then shows us to our table. He takes our drink orders and then leaves the table for us to look over the menu.

"He seems nice," Nik says.

"Yeah, he is. It's nice that he's working right now, he usually only works in the evenings. People used to joke that he was a vampire."

"A vampire?"

"Yeah," I say with a smirk. "I used to work with his girlfriend, Reese, but I haven't seen her around in a long time."

"No, wait, go back to the vampire thing. What do you mean?"

I chuckle. "We were just joking."

He gives me a bit of a frown but then nods and turns his attention to the menu in his hands.

"These all sound amazing, how am I supposed to choose?" he asks.

"You could get two pizzas, and take some home."

"Will you also get two pizzas? And then we can share each other's and we can each try four."

I laugh. "Sure, that sounds fun."

I want to ask him what it is about us that he's not sure about. I don't want to sound like I'm pressuring him or even shaming him for wanting to go slow, but he didn't exactly use those words last night, and I want to be sure we're on the same page. He said that he feels out of his element, but he also said there was something else and he couldn't tell me what it was. I'm enjoying getting to know him, but I'm afraid that he's going to drop some big bombshell on me that's going to make me not want to continue a relationship with him. I don't know what that would be, but what if it's something bad? No, of course it isn't something bad.

"Are you okay?' Nik asks me, pulling me from my thoughts.

"What? Of course."

"Okay. You just seem… somewhere else."

I look at him for a second, trying to come up with something to say that doesn't make the situation uncomfortable, when Felix comes back to our table. He just perfectly fit himself into the quiet space of our conversation before I had to think of a response for Nik, and I silently thank him for it.

"Are we ready to order?" Felix asks.

I walk up the stairs to Nik's apartment with him, each of us with a cardboard pizza box in our hands. I want to go into Nik's apartment with him, talk about us, but I also want to see Brett and Olivia. We stop in front of his door and he turns to me, probably also unsure about how to continue our afternoon.

"Thanks for taking me to all the cool places in town," he says softly.

"No problem. Thanks for coming with me. It's been fun."

"Yes, very fun."

"I think-" I start to say, but then Nik says something at the same time.

"Do you want to come in?"

"Oh," I say.

"Sorry, you were going to say something."

"No. I was just. I was going to say that…" I trail off, because I do want to go into his apartment with him. I want to go in so badly, but I also want to visit with my brother and niece. But it's only 2:30 in the afternoon; I have all day to go see Brett and Olivia if I want. "I was going to ask you if anything magical happened in your apartment last night."

He lets out a small laugh. "What?"

"Did you find anything? Out of place?"

"I don't know what you mean."

"Come on, Nik," I half whine. "Nothing Christmasy?"

"Oh you mean my Elf?"

I turn a little and look back at Brett's door, afraid that Olivia might hear us if she's near the door. I turn back to Nik and grin at him, and he smiles at me. "Yes, your elf," I say quietly.

"Do you want to see?" he asks.

"Sure."

We take our wet boots off and place them beside the door once we get inside. After putting our leftover pizza in the fridge, I follow him to his room to see the magic that I created for him. His elf is still sitting on his dresser, his little rubber fingers that are stuck in a permanent C position clinging on to the edge of the open pocket watch.

"Ah! He's learning to tell time!" I say.

"Is that what he's doing?"

"Of course! What a cutie."

"Did you move him?" he asks me quietly.

"No, of course not! He's magic! That's why you can't touch him, or it ruins his magic and then he can't go visit Santa in the North Pole!"

"Morgan," he says slowly.

"What?"

"I know how it works."

"Everyone knows how it works," I say. "I'm just trying to have fun."

"Olivia doesn't know how it works."

"That's because she's a child. All adults know how it works. And most children over the age of nine, probably."

This is when he tilts his head at me, his eyebrows sort of twisted in confusion. "What do you mean?"

"What do you mean what do I mean?" I ask him. "How old were you when you stopped believing in Santa?"

Stopped believing in Santa? *Stopped believing in Santa?* You're telling me that a child believes in Santa and then *stops*? Why do they stop? What makes a child just stop believing in Santa? In me? It must be because of things like this elf that their parents move. Children must find out that parents are lying to them about their magical Gingerbread Elves and so they must think that everything else is a lie too.

But wait. Is this not what made me stop delivering presents in the first place? Parents were using the same wrapping paper on gifts from them, and gifts that they *said* were from me but weren't. So they're buying the presents that they're pretending are from me, they're moving the toys that they're saying are moving because of Christmas magic, or sorry, *Gingerbread Magic,* and they're eating cookies and telling their children that they were eaten by me. This is all something children would definitely eventually catch on to, especially if they hear their parents talking about it, or catch them in the act. But what I still don't understand, is why? Why are they going to all this trouble when they literally wouldn't have to lift a finger if they just let me do it instead, like I've been doing, or trying to do, for the last fifteen hundred years!

And if this is all about no one believing in me anymore, why would people pretend that I exist and then also trick their children into believing their supposed lies?

"Nik?" Morgan puts her hands on my shoulders, and I try to look at her, but the room is spinning. If I try to focus on her, she just spins around me like everything else.

I try to take a deep breath but I can't. I have no idea who I am anymore. Even on my journey here, I thought I was getting to the bottom of a mystery, finding out why people are doing my job for me so I don't disappear, but now it feels like I already have. Or like I've never existed in the first place. Am I even real? Am I a figment of everyone's imagination? I take a step back and feel the backs of my legs hit my bed, so I sit down. Morgan kneels in front of me and puts her hands on my thighs, which feels nice, but not nice enough to stop this horrible feeling.

"Are you okay?" she asks, looking up at me.

I gulp and shake my head. I close my eyes, hoping that will make the spinning stop, but my heart now feels like it's going to break through my ribcage. I put my hand on my chest and try to take another breath but I can't seem to get any air. No matter what I do, my breathing isn't working.

"Slow down," Morgan says in a soothing voice. Slow down? I'm not even doing anything.

I try again to take a breath and I just about fall over, but Morgan grasps my arms and keeps me up.

"You don't have to tell me what's going on," she says, "but you have to try to calm your breathing."

Calm my breathing? I'm not breathing at all, am I? I'm trying and it's not working.

Oh.

I nod my head at her, but I can feel tears stinging my eyes and I'm embarrassed. The last time this happened, my reindeer were the only witnesses, and I didn't care about impressing them. Plus I've known my reindeer forever, and it's less weird having a panic attack in front of someone you know really well.

"Tell me five things you can see."

"What?" I ask through a gasp.

"Right now, in this room, what are five things you can see?"

Her hand slips into mine and she squeezes it, making me feel a little safer.

"Um," I start, gulping. "You?"

"Okay, good, that's one. Four more things."

"My dresser," I say, my voice unsteady. I look around my room, not even sure what I should be mentioning. There are so many things in here. "The elf doll."

"Good," Morgan says. She squeezes my hand again and I squeeze it back.

"My clothes hanging in the closet."

"One more."

"I…" I take another deep gasping breath, trying to focus on things in my room like she told me to, but I can't. "Um," I try.

"What about your pocket watch?" she asks.

"Right, yeah, that. My pocket watch."

"Okay, now name three things you can touch."

"Uh." I'm trying. I want to focus, but I can't. "Your hand."

"Good."

"My… My bed."

She nods and smiles, looking up at me from her position on the floor.

"Your shirt," I say with a bit of a gulp, gripping her hoodie sleeve with my free hand. I take another breath but it seems to be less intense this time. My breathing has softened to something closer to normal, but I don't know when that happened.

"Any better?" she asks.

"A little." I nod and look away for a second.

"You did it," she says.

"I'm really dizzy," I manage to say.

"You should lie down."

I nod and Morgan stands up as I start to lie back on the bed, my legs hanging off the end.

"Do you have experience with this?" I ask her.

"No," she says with a shrug. "I just though that panicking wouldn't help the situation and I've heard of that, so I gave that a shot. I don't even know if we did it right."

"Well, it was helpful. Thank you."

"Of course. Do you want to tell me what happened?"

"I had a panic attack."

"Yeah, I figured that much. Why?"

"I don't think I can tell you."

"Not this again."

I'm feeling a little better so I sit up, but keep my elbows locked and arms stretched out behind me, so that I'm propped up a little. "I'm really sorry to keep you in the dark, but if I tell you what's going on, you won't believe me."

"Is it the same thing that made you unsure about kissing me?"

I let out a deep breath. "Yes."

"Okay. Well, the only way to know if I'll believe you is to tell me."

"I want to. Oh, I want to tell you so badly, but I can't."

"Is it something bad?" she asks.

"No, not at all. At least, I don't think it is. You just *really* won't believe me."

"Are you a vampire or something?"

"W-what?" I stammer.

She stares at me with intense eyes and then she smirks and lets out a raspberry as if she's trying not to laugh. "Sorry. That was supposed to be funny, but it was stupid."

I chuckle and shake my head. "No, not stupid."

"I really like you, Nik. And I want to keep getting to know you. But I don't know if I can if you're already refusing to tell me things. Especially things that are keeping me from fully understanding you. Like, if this is the reason you're not sure we should be pursuing a relationship, I think I should know what it is. And then we can decide together."

"That sounds really logical."

"Great. So tell me."

She sits next to me on the bed and reaches for my hand so I sit up straighter and let her link her fingers through mine. I look into her brown eyes and try to imagine telling her who I am. That I'm Nikolaos of Myra, St. Nikolaos. Santa Claus. I imagine her eyes lighting up and her smile reaching across her entire face, and I imagine her kissing me. It's wonderful. I run my fingers through her hair and she messes mine up, and we spend the rest of our lives together.

Whoa. That's a little intense. I've only just met her. We've only spent two days getting to know each other, and already I'm imaging spending the rest of my life with her? And what kind of a life would I want? Would she come back to the North Pole with me? Surely not. Would I stay here? That wouldn't work, because who would deliver the presents? But then I remember that no one needs me to deliver presents, and if everyone continues to do it for me, and if they continue to allow their children to believe I don't exist by the time they're ten years old, I will surely start fading away very soon. And then none of this will matter anyway because I probably won't be alive.

"I'm in a real bind, here," I say quietly.

"Let me help." She shimmies closer to me and my breath hitches at the thought of her leaning in to kiss me or something.

"I've met a few people since moving here," I start, not entirely sure where I'm going with it. "Adults. Adults who I think believe in Santa."

"That's a weird thing to say."

"You said that no adult believes in Santa Claus, but I know I've met some who do."

"They were playing along, Nik. Like I was trying to get you to do with the elf. Because it's fun. Like you said you did every year where you used to live."

"That was different."

"I don't understand why this is such a big deal," she says, letting go of my hands.

"I wish I could show you," I whisper, leaning into her.

"Show me what?" She presses her forehead against mine and I can feel her breath on my lips.

"That I'm real." I wish that I could kiss her. I want to press my lips to hers and pull out her braids so I can run my fingers through her hair. But I can't do that to her. I have no idea if her feelings for me are even real. What if she only feels comfortable with me because of my magic? What if *I* only feel comfortable with *her* because of my magic? I'm drawn to her in a way I've never felt before, and I don't know what to do about it. I have no idea what's real anymore.

"Of course you're real," she whispers, her sweet breath on my lips.

"If only you knew."

She brings her face closer to mine, slowly, as if she's asking for permission. I let her, but I don't close the gap between us. She brings her mouth closer to mine, and our lips are almost touching.

"Can I kiss you?" she asks.

"I don't know if that's a good idea."

"Right. Sorry. You're right. I'm really sorry." She stands up and takes a step back.

I want to say something to her, but I don't know what. It looks like she's fighting the same battle, her mouth opening and closing a few times with no words coming out. Like she keeps changing her mind on what to say.

"I wish there was a better way for me to explain this all to you," I finally say.

"I don't understand why you can't just tell me. Just tell me straight, Nik."

"I told you, you won't believe me."

"How do you know?"

"Because you just told me that you don't."

"What?" She blinks a little and almost steps back. "What do you mean? No I didn't."

"You did. Before my panic attack."

"What?"

"You keep saying that," I say.

"I'm just- I don't- I don't understand what you're saying. Hang on." She puts her hands on her hips and circles around the floor at the end of my bed a few times before stopping and looking at me. "What?" she says again.

I try to not laugh, and it comes out as a weird exhale. I stand up but don't move closer to Morgan. Instead I just shove my fists in the front kangaroo pocket of my hoodie and let out a deep breath.

"I still don't know everything that I want to know, but I know enough to know that you're going to leave as soon as I tell you the thing," I say.

"First of all, that didn't make sense. And second of all, you're being ridiculous. Whatever it is, I don't care. Has it been a long time since you've had sex? Because I don't care. That's a weird thing to care about."

"Well, I mean, it has been a long time, but that's not what the thing is."

"Okay."

I let out another breath and she just stares at me. Well, I guess this was fun while it lasted, but it's over now.

I let out a breath and just say it. "I'm Santa Claus."

CHAPTER 10

"Fine, don't tell me," Morgan says. "But I'm leaving."

"What?"

"I'm 35 years old, Nik, I don't have time for this. And I know you said you wanted to take things slow, which I'm totally okay with, I love taking things slow, but not like this!"

"Not like what?"

"With you lying to me or giving stupid excuses as to why you can't be with me! I'm okay with just being your friend, but if that's all you want, you have to tell me."

"I would love to be your friend," I say quietly.

"Okay," she says slowly.

"And I would love to be more than that, too."

She groans and tilts her head back. "Oh my god, Nik! I can't do this."

She starts to turn away but I grab onto her arm, pulling her back.

"Wait," I tell her. "I'm not lying to you. Or making excuses. I feel really comfortable with you too, but the reason that I wasn't sure at first, was because I didn't know if it was real. I was afraid that you only liked me because of who I am, and how I naturally make people feel, and I didn't want to take advantage of you. I still don't."

"You're not making any sense!"

Both of us are startled by a "Yoo-hoo!" coming from my front door. Our heads snap towards the hallway and when the voice continues, I'm sure that I've been saved.

"It's December! I thought I would come see how everything was going!" Charlie calls from the hall. "Where are you?"

"Who's that?" Morgan asks.

"Charlie."

"Your best friend?"

"Yes."

"Okay, then I will let you two catch up-"

But she's interrupted by Charlie making his way into my bedroom. He's wearing jeans and a green hoodie, which looks a little strange to me, but I guess he needs to disguise himself too. His ears are still pointy, though. I wonder if he knows. "There you are," he says, but then his eyes fall on Morgan and he stiffens a little. "Oh. Hello." Without missing a beat, he grabs his hood and pulls it over his head, covering his ears.

"Hi," Morgan says. "I was just leaving."

"No, please, stay," I say.

"I'm sorry, Nik, but I'm going."

I let out a sigh and watch her leave through my bedroom door. I listen for the door into the main hallway of the building to close and then I turn my attention back to Charlie.

"Who was that?" he asks.

"Morgan."

"Oh, that explains everything," he says, his response dripping in sarcasm. He grabs his hood and lets it fall back behind his head again.

"You didn't ask me to explain everything; you asked me who she was."

"I thought that asking who she was implied that I wanted to know more."

"If you wanted to know more, you should have asked!" I don't mean to raise my voice, but I'm so confused and frustrated that it happens almost without my permission.

"Are you okay?" Charlie asks, his voice softened.

"No. I'm actually not." I let out a deep breath and sit on the end of my bed.

"Are you going to tell me why you're not okay? Or more about that Morgan person?" He gestures his head to the door, as if Morgan is still there, and I see his eye catch on the elf doll on my dresser as he brings his gaze back to me. "Or what this weird doll thing is? Why does it feel like he's staring into my soul? What's wrong with it's feet?"

I let out a small chuckle and stand again so I can pick the elf doll up.

"His name is Charlie," I say with a smile. "After you."

"Oh. That's nice." But it doesn't sound like he thinks it's nice.

"He's a Gingerbread Elf," I explain.

"That explains nothing."

I sigh, which I seem to be doing a lot of lately, and put the elf back on my dresser. "People don't believe in me anymore, Charlie. And parents make up elaborate stories and illusions to make their children believe in me, and then allow them to grow out of it when they're older."

Charlie raises an eyebrow at me. "Grow out of it? Why in the name of Rudolph would they grow out of it?"

I shrug. "I have no idea. I don't know why parents try so hard to get their kids to think everything is real, either."

"But everything *is* real."

"Not all of it," I say. "This elf isn't. Parents put these elves in different places in their homes every night while their children are sleeping, making them believe that they got into trouble during the night and this is where they're stuck for the day."

"That literally makes zero sense."

"Apparently the elves report to me every night on the kids' behaviour, then they come back and do something mischievous, but they get stuck there during the day and children aren't allowed to touch them or they'll lose their magic."

"That's the most ridiculous thing I've ever heard."

"I know. But the little girl who lives across the hall, Morgan's niece, loves hers. She thinks it's the most magical thing in the world, and Morgan said that she thinks moving the doll when she's asleep is magical too. And you know what? She moved my elf doll when I wasn't looking, and it made me feel warm and fuzzy inside. A big part of me wanted to believe it moved on its own."

"Why have we not heard of these?" Charlie asks.

"Because no one asks for them for Christmas. Parents just buy them at Costco and tell their children that I sent them."

"Well this is more information than we had before you came here, so this is a start, I suppose."

"I suppose," I say. "Although I'll admit it has just made me more confused as to why people are doing things like this. Thinking I'm not real but making their kids believe that I am."

"Yes, it is strange."

"And I just told Morgan who I am and she didn't believe me."

"Well of course she didn't believe you, you look like that!"

"You're the one who told me not to look like myself!"

"Right, because I didn't think people would believe you!"

"But you thought they would believe me looking like this?" I gesture to my body with my hands.

"I don't know, I've never done this before!"

"That's what I said!"

We both sound panicked, so I grab onto Charlie's hands and we look into each other's eyes.

"We need to calm down," I say.

"You're right. Do you have any hot chocolate?"

We sip our hot chocolates in silence, leaning back against opposite counters in the kitchen. We glance at each other every so often, but we don't say anything. I don't know what to say. I don't know how to fix this.

"I like your tree," Charlie finally says.

"You can't even see my tree."

"I saw it when I came in. It's very cute."

I nod, and put my mug in the sink. "I'm going to cease to exist."

"We don't know that," Charlie says slowly.

"I need another hot chocolate."

"Oh, excellent, then I'll also have another. Can you put more marshmallows in it this time?"

I smile and shake my head at him, but I want more marshmallows in mine too.

Charlie snoops in my living room while I make the next batch on the stove, making sure the milk doesn't burn. Once I pour it into our oversized mugs and fill them with so many mini marshmallows that the hot chocolate almost spills over the side, Charlie has sufficiently examined all of the Christmas DVD and Blu-Rays I've picked up since moving here.

"Won't any of these explain things to us?"

"Well, they're fiction, Charlie, so not necessarily. And I've only watched two of them so far."

"Two? But you've been here for over a week."

"Yeah," I sigh. "I've been exploring. And I'm always really tired when I get home, so I haven't really had time. But the two that I watched explained nothing. One of them had what I think was supposed to be a fake Santa for some reason, and no appearance of real Santa, but he did bring a little boy a rifle."

"A rifle? That sounds like a terrible Christmas gift."

"It took place in the 40's and it was just an air rifle."

He half nods at me. "Ah."

I hand him his hot chocolate and he takes it gingerly in two hands. "Anyway," I continue, "the other one had real Santa in it, except that nothing was accurate, and it also didn't help. No one believed in Santa but then an Elf and his teenager friend helped everyone believe."

"How did he do that?"

"He read Santa's List."

"Santa's List?"

"Yes. Apparently it's a thing."

"A thing where?"

"Everywhere. There's a song about it."

"About a list?"

"Yes. Apparently I check it twice."

"Wait, a list of what, though?" Charlie asks.

"What children want for Christmas. Or if they're good or bad, I don't remember."

"Of all the children in the world who celebrate Christmas?"

"Apparently," I say again.

"And you check this list twice?"

I just give him a nod.

"But that would take forever!" he half screams.

"I know!"

"And who writes this list? How many pages is it? Do *you* write it? If you already know about all the children, why in the snowflakes would you need to write it down?"

"That's what I said!"

"Oh, we need to watch more of these." He puts his mug on the coffee table and picks up one called *Christmas Vacation*.

Well that movie didn't help. It made us laugh, which was fun, but nothing beyond that. We watch four more movies, two of which have mention of Santa but nothing more, and two that feature Santa or the North Pole heavily, but are completely wrong.

"Can we watch the movie where the elf made everyone believe in Santa in the end?"

"Sure, but I'm telling you, it won't help."

Charlie laughs with me throughout the movie, and every time someone talks about the elf being weird for thinking he's an elf, he opens his mouth to say something, but then never ends up making a sound. When the movie's over, we sit in silence for a few minutes.

"People in the movie were acting like the idea of Santa being real is ludicrous," he says.

"Yes. And Morgan acted that way when I tried to tell her who I was. She moved my elf doll for me and pretended it was real Christmas magic making it move, but when I told her I'm basically Christmas magic, she accused me of making it up. Of avoiding the real reason I can't be with her."

"Which is?"

"I don't know if she's actually attracted to me, or if it's just my magic that's doing it!"

"Ah, yes, that is a difficult situation. But why are adults befuddled at the idea of Santa existing, but trying to make their kids believe that he does? Uh, that *you* do."

"That's the part that doesn't make sense. Why are they lying about it? And going to great lengths to do it? If they all think I'm dead and want to keep my tradition alive, that's fine, that makes sense. But they shouldn't be pretending to be me in that process."

"Maybe that is all they're doing."

"What do you mean?" I ask.

"Maybe they think you died. And they loved what you did for everyone, so they keep your spirit alive by continuing what you did."

"Yes. I already said that makes sense. But playing elaborate pranks on their kids to make them think it's real? That it's actually me and not their parents? Why not just keep up with traditions without the pretending? And why make up new things? Like the elf doll, and the list? Also I didn't die! I'm still here! I've been here the whole time, so why would they think I died!? I never stopped delivering presents!"

"I know this is scary, Nik, but we'll figure it out."

"No we won't!" I stand up from the couch in frustration and grab at my hair. "We won't figure it out, and I'm going to disappear forever and then I actually will be dead!"

MORGAN

"Yeah, he did seem like a bit of a nutjob," my brother says to me when I tell him a brief story of what happened.

"Okay, he's not a nutjob," I say, a little defensive.

"I'm sorry, I thought you were complaining."

I sigh. "I *am* complaining. But I don't think he's a nutjob. That's a little harsh."

"You think?"

"Well. Yeah. You don't?"

"Morgan. The guy thinks he's Santa."

"Right."

"Who thinks he's Santa?" Olivia asks, walking into the kitchen to see us at the table.

"No one," I say, but then try to recover with, "wait, what do you mean?"

"I heard you two talking, you said 'he thinks he's Santa.'"

"Oh. You must have misheard us, sweetie," Brett says. "I said that he winks like Santa. Very magical."

"Who winks like Santa?"

"My new friend who lives across the hall."

"Oh yeah, he does wink like Santa." She stands up straighter as she smiles, like she's proud of herself for agreeing with us.

"Have you even seen him wink?"

"No, but I don't have to." She shrugs and turns to go back to her room, but I bend down and gently grab on to her waist and spin her back around to face us.

"What do you mean?" I ask her.

She shrugs again. "I just think he looks like Santa."

"The man who lives across the hall?" Brett tries to confirm.

"Yeah."

"But sweetie, he doesn't look anything like Santa." Brett grabs onto her hands and holds them between his.

"Yes he does! I guess he doesn't really *look* like him, but he does *feel* like Santa!" She sounds so excited, I want to be excited with her, but I'm just more confused.

"Well, he is very friendly," I say.

"Yeah." She slips her hands from her dad's and hops away. We both let her go this time, and then look at each other, perplexed.

"I wonder what would make her say that," Brett whispers.

"I have no idea."

"Well at least you sold an original painting out of this whole weird situation. That's pretty cool."

"Yeah, I guess. But now I have to bring it to him."

"No you don't," Brett says with a shrug. "Just wrap it up and leave it in front of his door. But I mean, you are bound to run into him with his door being literally four feet from mine. There's going to be awkwardness no matter what."

"But you don't think he's dangerous?" I ask.

"Dangerous? Morgan, the man thinks he's Santa Claus. I think the worst thing he would do is break into your apartment and leave something for you. Which, now that I think of it, is still super creepy."

"Yeah," I say with a sigh.

"Why don't you stay here the next few days? Olivia would love it. We can watch Christmas movies."

"Why don't you guys stay with me? Then we won't have to accidentally run into him."

"That's a better idea. Let me go tell Livvy."

Olivia's so excited to have sleepovers at my place for the rest of the week, and I go through their fridge for perishables to take with us while Brett helps her pack. I look through the peephole before stepping into the hall to make sure he's not out there, which he isn't. But as we stomp down the stairs together, I can't help but feel disappointed. A part of me wanted to see him, to talk to him again. I'm sure I just misunderstood what he was telling me and I'm blowing this way out of proportion. I mean there's no way he told me that he's Santa. He must have used it as some kind of comparison and I didn't hear him right, and now he's the one who thinks I'm the nutjob.

Right? He's so perfect otherwise. There's no way.

"Meet you there?" Brett asks once we get to the parking lot.

"What?"

"Both our cars are here. So… meet you there?"

"Oh. Right. Yes. Sorry. I'm all frazzled."

He smiles. "No worries. Let's go, Olive."

"Hey!" Olivia giggles. "Olives are for eating!"

"I know!" Brett jokes as he picks her up. "And you're just so scrumptious!" He pretend-nibbles on her cheek with exaggerated sound effects and her laugh carries across the recently plowed tarmac. I've seen them do this exchange before, and knowing that it's a thing of theirs makes me happy.

I continue to watch as he gets Olivia in the car and helps her buckle into her seat, and I almost turn around and go back into the building. Almost. But this is probably a good idea. Even if Nik isn't a nutjob and doesn't actually think that he's Santa Claus, putting a bit of distance between us is probably a good thing. I started falling way harder and faster than I've ever fallen for anyone, and that can't be a good thing. I let out a breath and watch the air puff out in front of me before I make my way to my own car.

We order pizza and eat it on the floor in the living room while we watch Christmas movies. I change the sheets on my bed so Olivia and Brett can sleep there, and when I come out into the hall, I catch Brett setting up sheets on the pull-out couch.

"Oh, thanks," I say. "You didn't have to help with that."

"Sure I did. Plus, I don't mind."

"Well I just changed the sheets in my room, so you and Livvy can have my bed."

"No, we're fine out here."

"I just changed the sheets, Brett, please take my bed."

He stops and smiles at me. "Fine. Thank you."

"Of course."

I grab a pillow for myself and bring it to the pull-out couch, and Brett gets Olivia ready for bed. I start washing the dishes and when Brett comes out, he grabs a towel and starts to dry.

"So what are you thinking?" Brett asks. "Do you think this was a good idea?"

"Yeah, definitely. Olivia's already having an amazing time."

"No, I mean, for you. Do you think that Nik guy is really dangerous?"

I sigh and lean forward, my soapy hands on the edge of the sink in front of me. "I don't know. This is all just really weird. What if I misunderstood him? What if he just really likes Christmas and I thought he was saying something he actually wasn't?"

"It is a little weird how much he likes Christmas though, especially for someone who doesn't even understand it."

"What do you mean for someone who doesn't understand it?" I ask.

"Well he came over the other day asking about how the Gingerbread Elf works. He thought it was supposed to move on its own."

"Yeah, he asked me about that, too. He's really oblivious. He was even confused about their gumball feet. I mean, it's right in the story." I shake my head, realizing that part isn't as important and now it just sounds like I'm making fun of him. "But he said that where he used to live, he played Santa for his whole town. They would donate money and toys for the cause and see him off every Christmas Eve."

"See him off?"

"Yeah, he delivered presents to people's doors."

"To everyone in his whole town?"

"He said it was a really small town. Way up North."

We look at each other for a beat too long, and I shake my head. "It does kind of sound like he thinks he's Santa Claus, doesn't it?"

"A little," he says with a bit of a wince.

"Do you think he made everything up?"

"I don't know, Morgan."

"Well let's just see how this week goes."

"Yeah. Of course."

I take Olivia to school in the morning, as I normally do, and then head over to my gallery. I park around the corner and get out of the car to start the short walk over. But as I'm heading down the sidewalk, I see someone standing in front of the door with his hands in his pockets. He's got a hoodie on, and the hood is bunched up around his neck at the opening of his red coat. For a split second I want to say he's Santa Claus, but that's ridiculous, of course he's not Santa Claus, and also Santa Claus isn't a 30-something-year-old man with dark hair and a short beard with lovely greys sprinkled throughout both. No, that would be Nik.

"Hi, Nik," I say as casually as I can.

"Hi," he says, seemingly a little hesitantly.

"What are you doing here?" I ask.

"I came to get my painting and I didn't want to bother you at home, or at your brother's. I never got your number after I got my phone, and I did pay for the painting, and I do still want it, and I thought getting it here was the best option, seeing as it's public?" He says it like a question, like he's unsure of my reaction, or if what he's doing is okay and he's looking for my approval.

"Yes. Um, that's- that was a good call. Thanks."

He smiles and gives a half nod, but it seems like he wants to say something else.

"Uh, come in," I say, getting my keys out.

"Thanks."

He watches me as I unlock the door and we both tap the snow off our boots on the concrete step before heading inside together. I slip my boots off and flick on all the lights. Nik watches me walk across my little store in socked feet and raises his eyebrows when I start to put on a pair of indoor shoes.

"Should I-" Nik starts, but I wave him off.

"You're fine, I just don't like wearing my boots in here all day."

He nods and I immediately start taking the painting down from the wall.

"Can we actually, um, talk?" Nik asks.

"Sure." I leave the painting and turn to give him my full attention.

"I'm really sorry if I freaked you out yesterday. I didn't mean to. I know what I said sounds absurd, but if you give me a chance, I can prove it to you."

"What do you mean?" I ask.

"I can prove to you that I'm Santa."

My eyes widen and I take a step back. "Excuse me?"

"I can take you there, I can show you."

I'm so nervous I don't even know how to react, and for some reason I laugh. I hate so much that I laugh. "Okay, I'm not going anywhere with you."

"But you went places with me this weekend." He actually sounds hurt.

"Yeah, that was before you revealed yourself as being, uh, whatever it's called when you think you're a magical being!"

"Okay, just tell me one thing."

"No, I think you need to leave."

"Why is it acceptable to pretend that an elf is learning to tell time in my apartment but not acceptable to pretend that I'm Santa?"

"What?"

"What's the difference?"

"The difference is it doesn't sound like you're pretending."

"So what if I'm not? What's harmful about Santa?"

"Nothing is harmful about *Santa*, Nik, but it's harmful when you believe you're something you're not!"

"Why?"

"Because!" I throw my hands up in the air and take another step back, almost into the counter behind me. "Because that's just the start! Believing you're Santa doesn't seem harmful, but what happens after that, if you think this is all real? Will you break into people's houses? Steal from stores as presents for people? Hurt people?"

"Why would I hurt people?"

"I don't know!"

"Why is it scaring you so much?"

"I just told you!"

"First of all, I don't *break* into people's houses. Why would they leave milk and cookies for me if they didn't think I was going to come in and eat them?"

"What?" I can hear my voice shaking and now I really wish I hadn't let him come inside with me.

"I'm invited in. Everyone knows that Santa shows up in front of everyone's Christmas trees every year, I'm not... I'm not breaking in." His eyes are red like he's trying not to cry, but I'm already crying. I wipe the tears away from my face and swallow hard.

"Stop it," I say. "Santa doesn't exist. And you are not Santa."

"But Santa never died," he says, almost a whisper. "He's still alive."

"Santa was never real, Nik."

"What?" And that's when I catch a tear seep out of the corner of his eye and roll down his cheek.

"Please leave. I'll wrap up your painting and have my brother deliver it to you."

"No, but-"

"Nik, please."

We're standing in my little gallery, splotchy faces and tear-stained cheeks on both of us, and I don't know what else to do.

"This- this doesn't make any sense," he says, his voice frantic. "I thought people just thought I died. Does everyone think I've never existed? Am I just a myth? What am I?"

"You're someone who is very kind, but who I think needs help."

"But Morgan. Didn't you feel- I mean, everyone can feel it. Kids, even adults, they've- they told me what they wanted for Christmas."

"Nik," I say again.

He raises his hands in front of him in a sort of surrender, and starts stepping backwards toward the door, but he keeps talking. "You felt it, that's why you were so comfortable with me. And you- you wanted a boyfriend for Christmas. You can't ask for a boyfriend for Christmas, but you probably know that, but now,

now it's a little fuzzy, and I can't- I don't- I don't know what's happening. What's going to happen to me?"

"I don't know, but you have to leave," I say quickly, trying to gloss over the part where he said he knew I wanted a boyfriend for Christmas. Like, I know I can't ask for a boyfriend for Christmas, but it's not like I'm being completely serious when I say that. Okay, maybe I'm being serious, but like, yeah, okay, I know I can't just ask for someone to fall in love with me as a Christmas present as if someone has control over that, I just want for someone to be able to have control over that. And give it to me. Like if someone *could* do that, wouldn't that be perfect? But no! It's not perfect, because I never told anyone that I wanted a boyfriend for Christmas and now this guy's acting as if I told him all about it! Is he some kind of mentalist?

"But- but the boyfriend-" he stammers, but I cut him off.

"Nik, please," I say, my voice cracking, because I can't deal with this anymore. I can't deal with him acting delusional, I can't deal with him somehow reading my mind, and I can't deal with the fact he's upset about it, as if any of this should be coming across as normal.

He nods and takes another step back, and then turns around and opens the door. He looks at me over his shoulder for a second before he leaves, the door almost slamming behind him. I let out a shaky breath and immediately lock the door.

And then I cry.

I don't know how long I cry for, but I'm light headed by the time I'm done. I don't know how to describe what I'm feeling. I don't think I'm afraid of Nik, but it breaks my heart to see him struggling like this. In a way that I know I can't help with. In a way that could potentially become dangerous if it isn't treated or handled properly. But I *do* feel comfortable with him. I do want to see where- no, I *did* want to see where this could go. I don't anymore. But it still makes me sad.

I go into the washroom in the back to make sure my mascara hasn't run everywhere. Of course it has, and I try to use some wet paper towel to clean it up, but it doesn't work very well. I go back into the gallery to grab some moisturizer from my purse when someone knocks on the door. I almost jump out of my shoes and take a second to compose myself before going to open it.

"Hi, sorry," I say, letting him in.

"No worries. I wasn't sure if you were open or not."

"Yeah. I was just in the washroom. Can I help you with anything?"

I step back to give him more room to come in, and then I feel awkward so I stand behind the counter.

"I'm new to town and I was just browsing all the shops down here."

"Oh, excellent. Well if anything catches your eye, I have prints of everything if you weren't looking to spend a lot. But also, no pressure."

"You don't remember me, do you?" he asks.

"I'm sorry, I guess I don't."

"I'm Nik's friend. Charlie."

"Oh. Oh my god, I'm so sorry. I only saw you for like a second, but yes, now that you mention it, I do recognize you."

"Yeah." He nods and puts his hands in his coat pockets.

"Sorry, if you're here to try and convince me to-"

"Oh no, he doesn't even know I'm here. And I'm not lying, I am just looking at all the shops in town, I didn't even know you worked here."

"I own it," I say a little sheepishly.

"I'm sorry?"

"I'm- I'm the owner," I say.

"Oh, is this all your art work?"

"Yeah."

"Wow. It's amazing."

"Thank you. Actually, are you going to see Nik again soon?"

"Yeah, why?"

"He bought this one here. Would you mind taking it to him? Because I don't think- Um, I mean I'm not- uh, I don't think I'll be seeing him again."

"Oh. That's a shame."

"Yeah." I sigh and we look at each other in silence for a few seconds too long. "It is," I add.

"Well, I will definitely take it to him. But can I ask what happened between you two? He seems to really like you."

"Yeah. And I liked him too. Or, I thought I did. But he's... Um, you know, I'm not sure I feel comfortable talking to you about this. I don't even know you."

"Oh. Sorry. Why don't I just take the painting and get out of your hair?"

"You're not in my hair." I shake my head a little. "But, um, yeah, that would probably be best." I hate how much I'm saying 'um'.

I take the painting off the wall and wrap it in brown paper before handing it over to him. He smiles and tells me to have a good day as he leaves. And as soon as the door is shut I wonder if giving him the painting was a bad idea. What if he doesn't give it to Nik? What if Nik demands a refund because he never got it? And then I'd be out a painting *and* $500. This was not a good idea. I'm about to get up and chase him down when the door opens again.

"Hey, me again," Nik's friend says. "Sorry to be a bother. But I do still want to keep looking around town, so would it be too much trouble if I left this here until I'm ready to head home?"

"Oh, of course. That's of course a reasonable request. I'm sorry I sort of threw this at you. Also you don't have to take it to him, I can just, um, my brother lives across the hall from him, so my brother can bring it to him."

"Nonsense. I'm staying with Nik so it makes sense for me to bring it. I just don't want to damage it."

"Right, of course." I meet him on the other side of the counter and take it from him. "Um, I'm here until 5:00."

"Okay, I'll be back before then for sure."

"Great."

I set the painting on the counter and watch him leave again. I take out my iPad and check emails, but I don't have anything new. I was hoping the brewery had a new beer coming out soon so I could start making up a label for it, but my inbox is empty. So I open Procreate and start making line drawings of Santa and elves and other Christmas things that I can print for Olivia so she can colour them later.

Nobody else comes into the shop for the rest of the day, which isn't unusual, but at 5:00, Nik's friend still hasn't shown up to get the painting. I decide to wait an extra ten minutes for him, but he doesn't show. I leave the painting on the counter and turn off the lights before locking up.

Snow falls in huge, fluffy flakes, and they glow under the soft light of the street lamps. I let the snow fall into my hair and smile up at flakes as they come down. White twinkle lights wrap around the posts of the street lamps, and some businesses have white or colourful lights lining their windows. I should put up lights around my window. I turn the corner to get to my car and almost bump into Charlie.

"Oh, sorry," I say, stepping back. "I waited for you, but I had to close up."

"Yeah, I'm really sorry, I tried to get here earlier. I was just thinking about you and Nik, and trying to come up with an explanation that you'll understand."

"An explanation for what?"

"For Nik. I know he told you about him being Santa, and if it helps, he hasn't gone by Santa for that long."

"Huh?"

"Yeah, a lot of people don't know that. The name Santa Claus is relatively new. It just sort of evolved, you know? But there are more people in the world now than there ever were before, and it was easy for him to go with the flow and call himself Santa Claus along with everyone else." He smiles at me and his voice is full of excitement, like he's been wanting to tell his story forever.

"Okay," I say, taking a step back. "That's really nice information. Thanks for sharing that, Charlie." Maybe if I'm polite, he'll be happy and then leave me alone.

"Yeah. He's accepted all of his names, actually. He's really good at adapting. Except when he thinks he's going to disappear into thin air, he's not good at adapting to that."

"I mean no, I wouldn't either," I say. Agreeing with him is the best option, right? Agreeing and walking away? "Anyway, I should go," I add. "But this talk has been nice."

"So you believe me?"

"Believe you?" I ask.

"About Nik."

"Oh. Um. Maybe if you took me to the North Pole, then I'd believe you," I say with a nervous chuckle.

"Really?"

My insides turn to ice and I look at him, about to shake my head. I open my mouth to say something like, 'not right now,' or 'I was joking, I actually need to get home', you know, something polite but that doesn't sound like I want him to grab me by the arm and force me somewhere I don't want to go. Which is what he's doing.

His arm is on mine in half a second and before I get a chance to voice any concern, he says in a gentle tone, "This might be a little disorienting."

What? What's going to be disorienting?

And then it feels like I'm spinning around so fast but my feet feel planted on the ground. I want to barf, but I also don't want to barf, you know? I scream and then almost as soon as it started, it goes away. I still feel nauseated though, and the spinning feeling still lingers a little, keeping me off balance. I feel like I need to fall flat on the ground immediately or my head will pop off.

"Are you okay?" Nik's friend asks me.

"No. No, I'm not." I let out a huge burp and slap my hands over my mouth, and that's when I realize that he doesn't have his hand on my arm anymore. "I'm going to throw up," I say, and immediately kneel in the snow beneath me. The wet cold seeps through my jeans and even just that helps a little, but I still lean forward, my hands sinking into the white frozen fluff, and retch.

"I'm sorry," he says.

I throw up in the snow once, and then dry heave, my body still retching and gagging on this spinning sensation. I need to lie down. I sit back on my bum, not even caring about getting it wet, and the spinning starts to ease up. I take a few deep breaths and try to ground myself before I yell at Charlie.

"What did you do?" I ask in a shout. And then I look around at the winter wonderland before me and gasp. "Where are we?"

"The North Pole."

"What?" I force myself to stand as if that will help me better take in my surroundings. Snow completely covers the trees in fluffy white blankets, and the houses and shops on either side of the footpath are lit with warm lights, giving them a comforting orange glow. The snow around the edges of their windows is lit by it all too, coming through like their own twinkle lights. The foot path looks like it's been shoveled recently, but there's a light layer of snow dusting it, as it's currently coming down around us.

"I took you to the North Pole. You said it was the only way to get you to believe."

"What?" I say again.

"I'm sorry, is that not what you wanted?"

"No, that's not what I wanted!" I shout. "Why would I want you to kidnap me?"

"I didn't kidnap you!" Charlie shouts back. "I would never do that! You said you would believe me if I took you to the North Pole!"

"Did I say I *wanted* you to take me there? Did I say, 'Charlie, person I literally just met, please grab my arm and drug me so that it feels like we've teleported to the middle of buttfuck nowhere'!? Did I say that?"

"Well, no, I- I don't think anyone would say *that.*"

"Then why did you do all that?" I tighten my hands into fists as I step toward him, making him take a step back.

"Because I misread the situation! And I didn't drug you! I would never drug you! And- and I need you to believe! I think you're the most important person in all of this!"

"In all of what?"

"People believing in Santa."

"What are you talking about?"

"Can I just show you around? Would that be alright?"

"No, that would not be alright! You kidnapped me! Take me home!"

"You keep using that word. I didn't- I didn't kidnap you."

"I don't care what word you want to use, but I don't want to *be here* anymore! So however you got me here, do that to take me home!"

"Yeah, sorry, I can certainly take you home. After I show you around."

"Uh, no, take me home now."

"Well I can't just up and teleport whenever I want."

"What?"

"It takes a lot of work, and I've only just figured out how to take someone with me when I do it, so I need some time before I can do it again. I had a lot of practice with furniture recently, but it turns out teleporting objects is not the same as teleporting humans. Humans are much more exhausting."

"What?"

"Can you say anything besides what?" he asks.

"No! I can't! Because you're not making any sense!"

"Oh I'm sorry, let me explain. I'm Charlie, Nik's oldest and best friend, and head elf of the North Pole. We're here in the North Pole because I thought you asked me to bring you here to convince you that Nik is Santa Claus, so I used my magic to teleport you here. See, no one seems to believe in him anymore, and we're afraid he's going to disappear into the void if this continues, but I think if you believe in him, it'll spark something in the rest of the world. Like the Christmas movies."

Tears start to well in my bottom lids and my head goes all wobbly. My vision starts to get dark around the edges and I think I might barf again. What is happening? Why am I attracting all the bizarros? What have I done to make them feel like they can share all of this with me? Nothing! I haven't done anything! I hold my hands out to my side to help keep my balance, and turn away from Charlie, into the rest of this weird, quaint, adorable little village. I almost get to the steps of a shop or a café or something when I can't hold myself up anymore and I fall into the snow and everything goes dark.

I wake up in a very comfortable bed. The pillow under my head is like a cloud, and the blanket over me is heavy and warm, but not suffocating, and even though I have no idea what's going on and I'm pretty sure I was kidnapped, I feel very safe under it.

"Hey," Charlie says in a soft voice. He's sitting in a chair across the room.

"Hi," I reply shortly.

"How are you feeling?"

"Like I was kidnapped and then threw up and then fainted."

"Okay, yeah, that's fair. I'm sorry, but I've never done this before."

"You've never kidnapped anyone before? Well there's a first for everything, I guess."

"Can you stop saying I kidnapped you? I didn't mean to."

"You kidnapped me by accident?"

"Yes! Because I thought you wanted to come here!"

"You don't take any time to make decisions, do you?" I ask.

"What do you mean?"

"I said one thing about going to the North Pole and you immediately tried to take me there."

"Here," he says.

"What?"

"Here, the North Pole is here, not there, because it's where we are right now."

I roll my eyes. "Sure."

"I'm sorry," he says quietly. "You sounded so interested in what I was telling you about Nik, and when you said to take you to the North Pole-"

"I did not tell you to take me to the North Pole. See, you don't even listen to people. You just want everything to go your way and you won't stop to make sure you're respecting other people or not in the process."

"You're right. I'm sorry. I wish I could take it back. I'm not used to talking to people who don't believe in all this, and I really thought you wanted to come here. So you could be convinced about everything."

"About everything?"

Charlie sighs. "I told you already."

"Ah yes, about Nik being Santa Claus."

"So you believe me now!?" He actually sits up in his chair a little and has a cute smile on his face, his eyebrows raised in happy anticipation.

"No."

But it's at that second that I notice his ears. They're super pointy. Like unnaturally pointy. I want to ask him about them, but that's rude, and he's probably insecure about it. I try not to pay attention to them, but then he raises one of his hands to his left ear and touches it gingerly with his index finger.

"Are you looking at my ears?"

"No," I say, looking away.

"No, it's good. Look at them. They're pointy because I'm an Elf."

"A Christmas Elf?" I ask with a sarcastic tone.

"No." He folds his arms in front of his chest and readjusts himself in his chair. "That would imply that I'm only an Elf on Christmas."

"Okay..."

"I'm an Elf all year. All the time."

"So you're, what? A North Pole Elf?"

"Yes!" He practically jumps out of his chair. "And I'm actually a few thousand years old. I know, I look much younger." He smiles as if he's proud of himself.

"Okay. I believe you," I say. "Take me home now."

"Really?"

"Yes. I believe that Nik is Santa and I will tell everyone I know that Santa Claus is real so that he doesn't disappear, okay? Just take me home."

He stands up and starts to walk over to me. "This is amazing! I have to tell Nik the good news!"

I think he's going to take the blanket off me, or help me out of bed or something, but before he gets to me, he turns to the door and leaves! I thought lying to him would make him take me back right away, but I guess I over estimated the success of this plan.

"Wait!" I say, throwing the blanket to the side and swinging my feet off the bed. "Come back!"

I open the door to chase after him, but my feet are bare, and the wind whips at my skin and cuts through my pyjamas. Wait, why am I wearing pyjamas? Did he change my clothes while I was unconscious? I close the door and look around the little cabin for some boots or a coat. But there's nothing hanging by the door, so I check the little wooden dresser at the end of the bed. The drawers creek as I pull them open, but they're completely empty. There's the chair that Charlie was sitting in, a little ottoman, my bed, a bookcase, and the empty dresser. It seems the only thing keeping this place warm is a crackling fire in a brown and red brick fireplace, with two stockings hanging from the mantel. Wait a second. Two stockings? I take them off their hooks and immediately slip my feet into them. They're too big to wear as socks on a regular day, obviously, but they're perfect if I don't want my feet to freeze while I run through the snow after the delusional elf man. They're knitted with a soft wool blend of some kind that hardly itches my skin. I smile at myself and open the door again. It's still pretty windy out, but I can take a little wind. I'm used to lake effect snow and wind chills that bring the temperatures down to 30 below. I'll be fine.

I tighten my silk pyjamas around my torso and hold them tight against my chest with my arms, and trudge into the snow. Of course the stockings fall from my calves immediately, but as long as I drag my feet, they won't fall off completely.

"Charlie!" I yell. "Come back!"

Pretty, old fashioned street lamps cut through the darkness around me, their glow lighting my way towards the town. Where was I? Why is that weird cabin so far away from everything?

"Charlie!" I yell again. "This isn't very elf-like of you! I don't think Christmas Elves kidnap people! Oh, sorry, *North Pole* Elves!"

But then I see two people in the distance, and one of them sounds like Nik.

"Oh my god, I'm going to be sick," I hear him say. He leans forward and I definitely hear him throw up. There must be some stomach bug going around. But since I seem to have it too, I can't catch it from him, so I keep walking, letting the snow seep into my stocking socks.

"Oh, good, we're all here!" Charlie says as I get closer and I'm sure he recognizes me.

Nik is on his hands and knees, wiping his mouth with the back of his mitt, and his face practically freezes in horror when he looks up and sees me.

"Morgan?" he asks.

"What's going on?" I ask in return.

"Charlie, what did you do?" Nik asks, getting to his feet.

"I was just trying to help!"

"By kidnapping someone!?"

"I didn't kidnap her!"

"Then what did you do?"

"I just transported her here."

"Without my permission," I cut in.

"That's kidnapping!" Nik cries.

"I thought I had permission!" Charlie screeches, clearly frustrated. "I misunderstood!"

Nik takes a few steps towards me and holds his hands out to me, as if he wants to grab onto mine. "I'm so sorry, Morgan. I promise I had nothing to do with this."

"Okay. How do I get home?" I wrap my arms around myself a little tighter as if that will stop the wind from slicing into me.

"Why are you out here in pyjamas? Where are your boots?" He takes his mitts off and holds them in his teeth while he unzips his coat.

"I didn't know she was going to follow me out here," Charlie says. "I mean, look at what she's wearing."

Nik stops for a second to glare at him and then he turns back to me and puts his coat over my shoulders. "Let's get you warmed up."

"Can we just go home?" I ask.

Charlie shakes his head. "Nah, I got nothing left. Not for a while, at least."

"What's that supposed to mean?" I ask.

"It's okay," Nik says, sliding his mitts onto my hands. He puts an arm around my shoulder, leading me back the way I had come. "Let's just get you warmed up for now."

As soon as we get back to the cabin, Nik sits me on the bed and kneels in front of me. He takes the stockings off my feet and winces when he sees how white my toes are. He blows in his hands and cups them around my right foot, pressing his warm skin against mine. It burns a little, and I flinch and pull back without meaning to.

"Sorry," he says. He keeps a firm hold on my foot, letting his warmth seep into it. It feels a bit better after about a minute, and my toes start to get pins and needles. I wiggle them under his fingers and I catch him smile for a split second before looking up at me.

"Is that better?" he asks.

I'm still so confused about everything and I almost can't find my voice, but manage to say, "A little."

He nods and slowly takes his hands away so he can blow in them again and do the same thing on my left foot. I wish the way he was touching me wasn't calming me so much, but he's so gentle. The way he gingerly grabs my foot and presses his hands around it, the look of worry on his face, it's all making me feel safe, like he actually cares about what happens to me. I know he had nothing to do with Charlie taking me here, so I suppose feeling comfortable with the way Nik is taking care of me isn't that wild of an idea, but I still try to distance myself from these feelings, because whether or not he's nice, he still thinks he's Santa Claus.

"Charlie, hand me some dry clothes, will ya?" Nik asks without looking away from me. I hadn't even noticed that he followed us in here.

I turn my head to see Charlie make his way to the dresser. "There's nothing in there," I say, just as he pulls out some flannel PJs. "Wait, no, that doesn't make any sense. I looked in all the drawers before I followed you and it was empty."

"Yeah, sorry, that's not how it works," Charlie replies, handing the PJs to Nik. "You need to have intention. Oh, here are some socks too."

Intention? Did I not have intention when I was looking for clothes? Or do I need to be intending to find something there instead of hoping to? Oh why am I even rationalizing this? This is absurd! All of this is absurd!

"Thank you," Nik says to Charlie, taking everything from him in one hand.

He puts the PJs on the bed beside me and starts to put the first sock on. Once it's on, he rubs his hands all over my foot to continue warming it up. He does the same with my other foot, and then he lets out a big sigh.

"I'm really sorry my best friend basically kidnapped you," Nik says. "I'm going to have a talk with him about that." Charlie opens his mouth to object, but Nik holds a finger up at him, again, without taking his eyes off me, and says, "Right now. Outside. While you put these dry, and much warmer pyjamas on."

"Okay," is all I can manage to say. Because really, what the fuck?

Nik and Charlie go outside and I wait for them to start talking before I get up and start unfolding the pyjamas. It's hard to hear them through the door, but I try to listen anyway.

"That's not what I meant!" I hear Nik shout.

"What was I supposed to do?"

"Nothing! You were supposed to do nothing!"

And then Charlie responds with something that I can't make out, so I step closer to the door. The floor creaks on my second step and I stop, hoping they didn't hear and suspect that I'm eavesdropping. I wait a second, but it seems they've stopped talking. Afraid that they're going to barge in, I cover myself with my arms. But then I remember I'm still wearing the silk PJs, although they are pretty wet. When I hear them start talking again, but still can't make out what they're saying, I decide to get changed.

Nik knocks on the door a few minutes later, and I'm sitting on the edge of the bed, waiting.

"Come in," I say.

The door opens slowly and Nik walks in with a pair of boots and an extra coat in his hands, followed by a very terrified looking

Charlie. His shoulders are hunched and his face is all long and sad. I'm not going to feel bad for him, though. He kidnapped me!

"Hey," Nik says gently.

"Hi," I say.

"Hello," Charlie says.

"Can I, uh, can I talk to Nik alone for a minute?" I ask.

Charlie straightens up a bit. "Oh. Sure. I mean, yes. Yes, of course."

Nik watches him back up out the door and quietly shut it. He turns to me and smiles, but it doesn't reach his eyes. He's uncomfortable too.

"Are you okay?" he asks.

I shrug. "I guess."

"Look, I'm really sorry about all this. I didn't even know he could do that."

"He just figured it out, apparently."

"You talked to him about it?" He raises an eyebrow in curiosity.

"Briefly."

"What did he say?"

"Didn't he tell you? I thought he was so excited to tell you that I believe you're Santa Claus." I try to sound mock excited, but I don't have the energy, so I think it comes out sounding pretty tired.

"Yeah, I somehow found that hard to believe. You were freaked out about it when I told you the other day."

"Yeah," I sigh.

"Tell me what to do."

"Turn back time?" I ask.

"That's impossible, unfortunately. But if you want, and only if you want, I can show you around? This is where I live."

"Where you play Santa every year?"

"Yeah, if you want to call it that."

"Nik, how did we get here?"

"Magic."

"Where are my clothes?"

"Uh, being washed."

"Why can't they be cleaned with magic?"

"Not everything can be solved with magic."

"No?"

He lets out a deep breath and gestures to the spot next to me on the bed. "May I?"

I nod once, and let him sit down. I turn a little to look at him, but he keeps his gaze fixed on the floor for a minute, before turning it to me.

"I know you won't believe me. I know this all seems impossible to you. But I *am* Santa. And I've been trying to figure out why everyone does my job for me every year. I used to be the one who got everyone their presents, but over the years, parents have been filling stockings for me. Eating the food they leave out. I was afraid the world was losing their belief in me and that I was going to fade away. Like, literally. So Charlie convinced me to disguise myself, I guess, and do field research."

"Field research?"

"Yeah. Find out first hand what was going on, and fix it. Hopefully before Christmas, but we knew there was a possibility it might take more than a year."

"And you just started this research when you moved into my brother's building?"

"Yes. And then… And then I met you. And I thought you would be able to help me understand everything but it honestly just made me more confused."

"Confused how?"

"Well we were under the impression that people thought I had died and wanted to continue my tradition by filling stockings. But then they were putting my name on presents, and eating most of the food they left out for me. Why would they leave food out for me but then eat it? And if it wasn't for me, why would it be on a special plate near the Christmas tree? And why would they eat half of it and then leave the rest there? And why are all the parents playing elaborate pranks on their children and telling them they'll phone me if they're bad?"

I can't help but laugh. He sounds so serious and concerned, but he has to be joking. He's really good at this. But then I realize that I'm still laughing, and he looks like he's about to cry.

"I'm sorry," I say. "I just can't wrap my head around this."

"Can you just explain it to me? It doesn't matter if you believe me or not, I need to understand."

"People don't think Santa is dead, Nik, because Santa isn't real. He's never been real. He's based off some guy from like a thousand years ago who put coins down people's chimneys and then he got commercialized over time and turned into what he is now."

"He's based off of me. I'm that guy."

"You're a thousand years old?"

"Closer to two thousand, I think. But I've sort of lost track."

"How would that even be possible?"

"Magic."

Right, because magic is the answer to everything, isn't it?

"Okay," I say slowly, looking for a polite way to get out of this. "Thanks for telling me your story. Can you take me home now?"

"We have to wait for Charlie to build up his ability to go back again. It could take a couple days."

"What!?" I screech. "A couple days!? People are going to be worried about me! Where's my phone?"

"Your phone is here somewhere, but it won't work. Not here. I mean, it'll work, like, you can turn it on and stuff, but you can't call anyone on it."

"Well how am I supposed to reach him? He's staying at my place with me this week in case you turned out to be a psycho and tried to kidnap me!"

"What? Really?"

"Yes!"

"Why?"

I stand up now and throw my hands in the air, because I don't understand how a man can be so fucking clueless. "Because you think you're Santa Claus!"

"I am Santa Claus!"

"No you're not! Santa isn't real!"

"Stop saying that or it might come true!" He stands up too and we stare at each other for a few seconds. "Please," he whispers. "Please just come with me. I'll show you. You can meet Rudolph."

"Oh, dear god." I sit back down on the bed and put my head in my hands. This is too much.

"Are you okay?" Nik asks.

"No. I'm not okay. I think I need a brain scan when I get home."

"Uh, I'm not sure what that is, but okay. If you think it's something you need, then I support it."

I chuckle and stand back up. "Okay. Whatever. Take me to Rudolph."

I slip my feet into the winter boots that Nik brought and am amazed at how perfectly they fit me. And not only are they perfectly my size, but they're the most comfortable boots I've ever had on my feet. How are they this comfortable? I take a couple steps and feel my jaw drop in surprise. It feels like I'm walking on marshmallows. Nik hands me the coat and I put it on. It's not as surprisingly comfortable as the boots, but it too, fits me perfectly. I zip it up and throw the hood over my head.

"Okay," I say. "Let's go."

He steps outside first, and I follow him into the dark, snowy night. This is probably the worst idea ever. I'm probably going to get murdered. Rudolph is probably secret code for something terrible. Like murder. *Come meet Rudolph! Surprise! Rudolph is the name of my machete!*

But as we walk silently through the soft and crunchy snow, towards the lights that make me feel warm inside, I feel safe. I'm not sure what it is, and why I'm not questioning it more, but there's something that just makes me feel like I'm in good hands. Maybe it's because Charlie the kidnapper isn't around. After all, Nik had nothing to do with this, and is almost as mad as I am about it. The wind has gone completely, and the air is still around us, with a few big snowflakes quietly falling into our hair.

"What is this place?" I finally ask.

"I told you already."

"Okay, well how did we get here?"

"Why do you keep asking me the same questions? Are you expecting different answers?"

"I'm expecting a sane answer," I say.

"I don't really know what you mean by that. Come on, this way." He tilts his head to the left and walks off the path that almost isn't visible anymore because of the snowfall. I follow him, but the snow out here is deeper, and my boots sink into it with every step. He looks back at me a few times to make sure I'm not falling behind, and every time he does, he gives me a warm smile. I don't smile back. I feel safe now for some reason, but I'm still mad.

We come to the edge of a forest and Nik whistles a few times. He looks back at me and tilts his head to the side, I guess telling me to come closer. I step in next to him, and he nudges my elbow with his.

"Here she comes," he says.

I'm not sure who he's talking about, but a big reindeer, bigger than I think reindeer are supposed to be, comes prancing towards us out of the trees. His antlers curve off his head and branch off into three sections, and his brown and white fur is a little long. He slows down as he approaches us and then huffs, the breath coming out making a white cloud in the cold in front of Nik's chest.

"This one's Comet," Nik says, petting his neck. "You want to pet her?"

"Her?" I ask, taking a hesitant step.

"Yeah."

"But he has- she has antlers."

"Yeah, both male and female reindeer have antlers."

"Really?" I ask.

"Yeah, and male reindeer shed theirs in the winter. If you see any around in the winter without any antlers, they're boys."

"So Santa's reindeer are all girls?" I ask.

"Yeah. Do people not know that?"

"I don't think most people do. But they always have antlers in the stories and movies."

"Well that's something they got right."

"I think they're usually smaller than this, though."

"Oh really." He doesn't say it like a question.

"Yeah, like her head is coming up to your shoulders, but in real life, they might come up to your middle."

"Morgan, this is real life," he says with a smile.

"Right. Yeah. You know what I mean."

"Okay," he chuckles.

"Also not every Christmas story uses actual reindeer. Most of them do, but sometimes they're just regular deer, like the kind they have where I live. These deer definitely look more magical."

He sort of shakes his head, like he's silently laughing at me, and pets Comet again. "You want to pet her?"

"Will she bite me?"

"No, definitely not. Just come up slowly."

I take another step, the snow crunching under my boots, and then another. Nik puts his hand back on her neck and she sort of nuzzles into his touch. He takes his hand away and holds it out to me, so I let him guide my hand to her fur. We pet her together, and I'm surprised at how soft her fur is. Nik takes his hand away and I keep petting her, and then Nik gently nudges me closer. It's a little scary being this close to a wild animal, especially one this big, and when she moves her head, it startles me and I squeal, stepping back. She seems startled too, and straightens up a bit, and then runs off.

"Oh," I say. "Sorry."

"That's okay. She's not upset or anything."

But then a soft red glow comes through the trees. It lights up the snow on the ground, and my skin as I lift my hand in front of my face.

"Ah, here comes Rudy," Nik says.

And I almost fall over. The reindeer that emerges through the trees looks just like comet, only this one is a little smaller, and she has more white fur than brown. But her nose. I can't even really see the shape of it, because it's so bright, the shimmering and sparkling light is all that comes through.

"Is this," I start, trying to find my words, "is this- is this Rudolph?"

"Yeah."

"Holy shit."

Rudolph gets closer to us, and her nose seems to dim a little. I can see the shape of it behind the brightness now, and it's the same shape as the other reindeer's nose. For some reason I thought it would be a big ball, like a light bulb. I want to boop it. I slowly raise my hand to her nose and stick out my index finger. She raises her head and now her snout is proudly up in the air, right in front of my face, showing off her nose like a prize. I press my finger to the front of her warm, soft nose.

"Boop," I say quietly, before I bring my hand back.

She pulls back slightly and then shakes her head a bit, before bowing it down and then pressing the side of her face into my shoulder. I lower my head so that I can press my cheek against hers, and the warmth comes off her fur like invisible steam. She lets out a breath and nuzzles into me more, and I can't help but giggle.

"She likes you," Nik says.

I pet her jaw and then raise my hand to her antlers, running my fingers along them.

"This is amazing," I whisper through a huge grin.

Nik smiles back at me. "I'm glad you're having a good time."

Nik takes me into his town, which is tiny and adorable. All the buildings are painted in soft colours and have gabled roofs, big shutters on the windows and big porches with thick posts and railings. Most of them have multicoloured twinkle lights around the windows or wrapped around the porch railings. Every little building and house has a wooden sign hanging beside their walkways, displaying who lives there or what the shop is. *Carter's House*, one says. *The Jingle Family* says another. Another sign says *Sandwich Shoppe* and another simply says *Hot Chocolate*.

"Do you live in one of these houses?" I ask.

"One of 'em."

"Is that where we're going?"

"Later we can, if you want."

I look over at the houses as we walk, and then back at Nik. "Okay."

He takes me up a little hill towards a much larger building, and as we get closer I can hear cheerful music and people laughing. This building doesn't have a sign out front, but the porch seems to go all the way around the building, and some people stand in groups under its roof, holding warm drinks that steam in front of them, taking sips from them between bits of laughter and conversation.

"This is where we have town parties," Nik says as he leads me up the steps of the porch.

"What's the occasion?" I ask.

He shrugs. "There doesn't need to be an occasion."

"Nik!" someone shouts from behind us.

We turn around from the doorway to see a young man with a red toque walking up to us.

"Hey, Stanley," Nik says.

"How was your trip?"

"Weird. It's nice seeing you, but we'll have to catch up later, okay?"

Stanley smiles and nods. "Of course."

Nik turns back to me and puts a hand on my lower back but then immediately pulls it away. "Sorry," he says.

"It's okay."

We step into the town hall, or whatever it is, and I'm immediately warmed. Instantly I'm cozy and comfortable, like I'm inside a childhood memory. Like I'm visiting it instead of reliving it, so instead of feeling like me as a child, it's like I'm watching everything happen all over again, from inside the memory as my adult self. But the feelings I had as a child are still inside me now, pulsing through my veins like magic waking up. I don't see myself as a child here but it seems as though I could see her any minute. Like she could come running from around the corner or the other side of the tree, laughing without a care in the world. Even though I don't see her anywhere, it's still as though I could reach out and touch her.

The garland strung from the rafters is filled with colourful twinkle lights, and sparkling snowflakes hang down from it that catch the light when they turn. I walk closer to the big Christmas tree in the middle that's completely decked out in lights, popcorn, beads, glass balls, and mini Christmas carousels. I'm so overwhelmed with a feeling of comfort and safety, which I didn't even think could be possible. How can feeling comforted be overwhelming? But it's like I'm not even real, like I'm walking through a dream instead. Tears prick my eyes, and when Nik stands next to me, I look up at him.

"Are you okay?" he asks.

"How does it feel like Christmas morning when I was six years old in here?"

He shrugs and smiles. "Magic."

"No, but like, it doesn't just look like it, it actually doesn't really look anything at all like how we decorated when I was kid, but it *feels* like Christmas. When I was little, Christmas gave me this feeling, like this physical feeling inside me. I felt it every time we turned on the lights in the tree, I felt it on Christmas eve, and I felt it all day on Christmas. Sometimes Boxing Day, too."

"What's Boxing Day?"

"You don't have Boxing Day here?"

"No. You mentioned it before; is it a Christmas thing?"

"Yeah, it's amazing! It's like second Christmas!"

"Second Christmas?" He tilts his head a little and his smile grows.

"Yeah! But anyway, let me finish."

"Yes, sorry," he says.

"I always got this feeling. A physical feeling in my chest, and in my arms, like I could literally feel magic running through my veins."

"Was it warm?"

"No, it wasn't warm. I don't know how else to describe it. It's not a feeling I ever got any other time. Oh no, that's not true, I got it on my birthday sometimes, too. But not as intensely. I wish I had a better way to explain how it felt, but it was amazing, and as I got older, the feeling got less and less intense, until one year, I just didn't feel it at all."

Nik frowns a little. "That's sad."

"Yeah. I haven't had this feeling since I was probably 13 years old."

"Really?" He sounds really upset about this.

"Yeah. Until now."

"Well that's great, I'm glad that you're feeling it now. But what made that feeling go away for you?"

I shrug. "Getting older, I don't know. Christmas is less magical as you get older, and eventually it's just another day with pretty lights and presents."

"Hmm." He furrows his eyebrows at me and then looks around at all the people dancing and laughing. I hadn't even really noticed how many people were in here until now. I was so mesmerized by the decorations and the feelings they were giving me, that I hadn't even seen how many people were here, having a good time themselves.

I look closer at some of the people and notice they've all got pointy ears. Their clothes are relatively normal, although probably a little more festive than I'd seen recently. Everyone's sweaters look hand knit or crocheted, and most of them have some kind of Christmasey design. Whether it be Christmas trees, or reindeer, or just snowflakes, they're all themed in some way. Some of them have tinsel necklaces, I think as a bit of a joke, and some of them are wearing Santa hats or elf-looking hats. The hats are real looking though, if that makes sense. They don't look made out of felt or dollar store material. They look warm, well made, and *worn*.

Am I... Actually in the North Pole? I mean, I know I met Rudolph a few minutes ago, but that could have been a gimmick. That could have been some kind of trick. Somehow. I didn't think it was a trick as I was looking at her, petting her, but after leaving and starting our walk over here my mind started to rationalize. There was no way I just met Rudolph. That's ridiculous. Rudolph isn't real. Reindeer with glowing noses don't exist! But then the night kept going and now we're here in a room full of dancing elves and I don't want to say it out loud, but I think this all might be real.

"I need to sit down," I say.

"Are you okay?"

"I don't know." I push past Nik and through the growing crowd of people – elves – and back into the cold outside. The air is crisp, and breathing it in helps a bit, but I still feel light headed. I stomp down the three steps of the porch and into the pile of the snow that's building over the walkway, and then I collapse into the snow bank. I sink into it a little, and some gets into the collar of my jacket, but the cold wakes me up a little.

"Is this too much?" Nik asks, standing over me.

I can't bring myself to say anything so all I do is nod. He holds out a hand for me so I grab onto it and let him pull me to my feet.

"Let's go somewhere quiet," he says.

I nod again, and walk next to him, taking deep breaths and trying to shake this uneasy feeling.

We come up to a log cabin with a wraparound porch – I don't know why I'm mentioning the porch, they all have wraparound porches – and Nik leads me past the sign out front that says *Nik's House*. He opens the door and we step into a warm room with a coat tree and a boot tray. Nik takes his boots off so I do the same, and he places both pairs next to each other before taking my coat and hanging it up with his. He opens the next door and leads me into the living area of his house, which smells like cedar and pine, and a little bit of something sweet. Cookies, maybe? It's very comforting. Nik sits down on his big couch, sinking into the cushions, and motions for me to sit too. I sigh and sit next to him.

"Are you alright?" he asks.

"I'm… Okay," I say slowly. "I'm okay but I'm also not okay. This is a lot."

"What's a lot? Just being here?"

"Yeah, but everything else too. Like this isn't supposed to be real."

"Why not?"

"Because I told you, Santa isn't-" I stop myself because clearly I'm wrong, and try to start over. "Santa has always been- I mean, once we're old enough, we're always told the truth. I mean, what everyone thinks is the truth."

"That I don't exist."

"Right."

"Why?"

"What do you mean why?"

"Well I do exist. And I never stopped delivering presents. Except for last year, I didn't do it last year."

"Why not?" I ask.

"Because everyone was doing it for me already. Had been for years. I felt like I didn't matter. Like I was disappearing."

"I wonder what made people start doing it themselves."

Nik's eyes widen. "Wait, you don't know?"

I can't help but let out a small laugh. "No, why would I know that?"

"Well you know all about how people celebrate Christmas now, and all the Gingerbread Elf things, so I thought you would know."

"I wish I could help you with that."

"Well how do I get people to believe in me again?"

"I don't think you can. You would have to bring literally everyone here and show them this for them to believe."

"Well I can't do that."

"Of course not. Why don't you just show yourself? On Christmas Eve? Let everyone see you with your reindeer?"

"I can't, time slows down so much for me on Christmas Eve, no one would see me."

"Time slows?" I ask.

"Yeah. Otherwise it would be impossible for me to deliver to everyone who celebrates Christmas in one night."

"Oh. Weird. When I was a kid, I just always assumed it was magic."

"It is magic."

"Right. Yes. Yeah, of course, I just never thought of *how*, I guess. Like it never occurred to me that magic would allow you to visit everyone by *slowing time*."

Nik shrugs, and I struggle for something else to say.

"Well it's getting late," Nik finally says. "And you've had quite a day. Should I walk you back to your cabin?"

I would love to go back to my cabin, except that it did seem a little isolated, away from the rest of the town. What if something happened to me? The thought scares me a little, but so does bunking with the guy I was afraid of only yesterday. Yesterday?

Maybe it was longer ago than that by this point, and I'm not afraid of him anymore, but still. It's fresh. "Um," I start. But then I don't know how to finish.

"Or not?" Nik asks.

"It's just a little far away from everything," I say quietly.

"Yeah, Charlie thought you might want to have some privacy."

"Oh."

"There's probably a cabin closer you could stay in."

"Oh," I say again.

Nik raises an eyebrow and it looks like he's trying not to smile. "Or you could stay in my guest room?"

"You have a guest room?" I ask.

"Yeah."

"Get a lot of guests, do ya?"

He smirks. "Not often, no. But I do have an extra room, with a made-up bed, if you'd prefer."

"Uh, yeah. Sure. Maybe that's a good idea. Just so I'm not alone."

"Excellent. And hopefully Charlie will be recharged in the morning and he can take you back."

I'm not entirely sure why, but it stings a little when he says that. I thought maybe he was going to go back, too. But that's silly. Why would he want to go back? He tried to tell me who he was and I basically laughed in his face. He's home now, where he's most comfortable, and with his best friend. His kidnapping best friend.

I give him a tight smile. "Yeah," I say. "Hopefully."

Nik shows me to my bedroom, which is small but warm. The bed is probably a Queen size, and the comforter looks like it's made of flannel. I'll have to take these PJs off if I want to be able to move around under that blanket easily.

"Uh, is there a shower I can use?" I ask before he leaves the room.

"Yes, of course." He stretches his arm out to show me down the hall, and after I step inside the room, he opens a closet and grabs a towel for me.

"The floors are heated, so your feet shouldn't freeze when you get out of the shower," he says to me.

"Oh, nice. And, do you have a t-shirt I could wear? That comforter in there looks really warm."

"Yes of course, I'll put one on your bed for you."

"Thank you."

"Of course." He nods once and leaves the room, pulling the door shut behind him.

Okay. This is totally normal. Just turning the shower on in Santa's house. No big deal. Just stepping in the shower. This is a basic activity. Most people do it every day! Don't mind me, just using Santa's shampoo. Santa's body wash. Like a totally normal person. It smells like candy canes and cookies. It's delightful. Oh my god, this is so weird.

Oh these heated floors, though. Oh my goodness gracious, I just want to lie down on them and sleep here! Besides the fact that the floor is obviously very hard, I think it would be a great idea to sleep here. I wouldn't even need a blanket! Well, I guess I still would, because sleeping without a blanket is impossible for me, even if it's hot. I need something to cover me. But still, you wouldn't need a particularly warm blanket. Oh my god, Morgan, stop going on about the floors and just go to bed!

There's a red t-shirt and a pair of green and red striped boxers on the end of the bed, along with the clothes I was wearing before coming here, folded and in a neat pile. My jeans, my sweater, my t-shirt, and my socks sitting on top, curled into a ball. I can't help but smile as I move them to the top of the dresser beside the bed, and then put the t-shirt and boxers on. Nik had pulled back the top corner of the blanket while I was in the shower, so I get under it and then pull the soft covers over my shoulder. My head sinks into the pillow so easily, and I almost fall asleep before I can even turn off the bedside lamp.

I think Nik is making pancakes. I roll over in bed and stretch, and take in a deep breath through my nose so I can smell the warm goodness. This bed is so comfortable, I really don't want to get out of it, but I know I should. I force myself to swing my feet over the edge and stand up, and then I force myself to get changed into my newly washed clothes. Charlie, or whoever undressed me, thankfully kept my bra and underwear on, but that means I don't have clean underwear. I turn them inside out and put them on again before pulling my jeans on.

Once I'm dressed, I fold Nik's shirt and boxers and make the bed. Totally normal behaviour. I always make the bed when I'm staying at someone's house, so Santa's house should be no different. Right?

Right.

I finger comb my hair and then start French braiding each side. Once I'm started on the second side, I step out of the guest room and into the kitchen to find Nik with a huge smile on his face.

"Good morning!" he says.

"Morning." I finish the braid in my hair and start wrapping my bright pink elastic band around it.

"You can do that without looking in the mirror?" he asks me.

I pull myself onto the bar stool that's on the other side of the island and nod. "Yeah. It's actually easier for me to do it without looking in the mirror."

"Weird."

I shrug. "I have to do it by feel. If I look in the mirror, it being backwards confuses me and I get all messed up."

"Oh. I guess that makes sense. How did you sleep?"

"Um, amazing, actually."

"Really? That's great."

"Yeah," I sigh.

"So I have some bad news."

"What?"

"Charlie doesn't feel like he can take you back yet. Maybe by the afternoon, though?"

I let out a deep breath. "Okay. This afternoon."

"But for now! I made pancakes!"

We eat the pancakes with maple syrup and whipped cream and chocolate shavings, and they're honestly the fluffiest pancakes I've ever had. I eat more than I normally would, and I don't even feel sick from the sweetness. We sip hot chocolate on the couch in front of his fire place, and then we go for a walk in the snow. It's still dark out, and it just occurs to me that the North Pole probably doesn't get any sunlight during the winter. I always pictured the North Pole being sunny and bright. But the lamps every few feet along the path, and the lights on all the houses giving a warm glow is more magical. It's cozy. Quiet.

"Is it winter here all year?" I ask.

Nik narrows his eyes at me but doesn't answer my question.

"Sorry, that was stupid. I mean is the snow always here."

"Oh. Yes. We're up in the mountains, technically, so there's always snow, even in the summer when it might be a little above freezing in the lower altitudes."

"How does no one ever find this place?"

Nik shrugs. "Magic, I guess." Then he looks up and points to the sky. "The Aurora is out," he says.

I tilt my head back to see colourful ribbons of pink and green light dancing across the otherwise dark sky. They pulse and move, and dance across the horizon, even behind the trees in the distance. I wish the trees weren't blocking the horizon though, so I didn't have to look up so much to see them.

"They're beautiful," I whisper. "Can we watch them for a bit?"

"Of course."

I don't even care about the snow; I lie down on my back so I can watch them dance above me without straining my neck. Nik lies down next to me and we just stay there like that, our arms and legs splayed out between us, watching the lights dance across the sky.

"Whatcha doing?" I hear from a bit of a distance, followed by boots crunching in the snow, getting closer to us.

"Just watching the Aurora," Nik says, sitting up.

I don't want to sit up, because I know it's Charlie, and I don't want to talk to him.

"So I practiced going back to Canada to make sure I had enough energy to go," Charlie starts, "and I did, but then after coming back, I'm pooped again. So I'm sorry, I probably shouldn't have done that, and I can take you back tomorrow, I'm sure."

I let out a loud and irritated sigh.

"I'm sorry," he says again.

"Sure you are."

"Really. I was only trying to help."

"Well you're not helping now," I say. "I'm trying to watch the Northern Lights and you're ruining it."

"Right. Sorry."

His boots crunch in the snow as he walks away, and I listen until I can't here it anymore. And then I sigh again.

Nik and I end up walking most of the day. We just stroll casually along the walking path, and I occasionally jump into a snowbank or throw a snowball at him. We have lunch at a café run by two Elves named Pikah and Andy. They make amazing sandwiches, but don't charge for any of the food. No one charges for anything here, apparently. Everyone does everything because they want to, and nothing but love and magic keeps everything running. Everyone trades for things or helps each other out, most clothing is handmade, and when it's gotten from a shop, it isn't purchased. It's just there for anyone who wants it. The shop owners keep track of what gets taken so they can see what needs to be replenished, but that's about it. I don't fully understand how it all works for everyone, even when Nik tries multiple times to explain it, but I guess it doesn't matter.

Nik tells me about the books he reads, and takes me to a book shop to show me. All the books are written and published by Elves here in the North Pole, and I take one about an Elf named Rusty who goes to space and gets lost, but turns out the secret love of his life is on the ship with him, and they try to find their way home together.

We walk back to Nik's house and he makes us Spaghetti with tomato sauce, smothered in freshly grated parmesan cheese. Once we've finished eating, we make our way to the couch. It's quiet for a few minutes before Nik says something.

"Tell me more about Box Day."

"Boxing Day?" I clarify. "It's just the day after Christmas."

"That's it? But when you talked about it before, it sounded like…" he trails off as if he's not sure how to finish.

"It's a holiday in most Common Wealth countries, I believe. So like, Canada, the UK, Australia…" I trail off too, because I'm not an expert and don't want to accidentally lie to him. "It started with rich families who had staff running the household. The staff worked Christmas so the family could have their holiday, but Boxing Day would be for the servants. The families would box up their Christmas leftovers and give it to the servants to have. And the day off, I think. I hope. Or the boxes had presents in them? I don't really know, actually, but I think it's something like that. But that's not what it's about anymore. Now it's just a holiday that's the day after Christmas. Some people go shopping on Boxing Day because the stores have good sales, and some people just use it as another day to spend with their families."

"Right, I remember you mentioning going to your grandparents' on Boxing Day to have Christmas again with the whole family."

"Yeah," I say with a smile. "And it's just nice to have that extra day after Christmas. You don't have to worry about getting ready for work the next morning and making sure you're going to bed early. You can stay up late on Christmas night and continue your traditions into the next day. And Boxing Day never really has any expectations, you know?" I shrug. "I don't know, I love Boxing Day. And now I spend it with Olivia and Brett. We make turkey sandwiches for lunch, and have turkey soup for supper, and we just spend the whole day in our PJ's, not unlike Christmas."

"That's great."

"Yeah."

It's quiet again and we stare at each other for an almost uncomfortable amount of time, except that it's not uncomfortable. It's so comfortable that I want to shift closer to him. Make him wrap his arms around me.

"Why is your name Nik?" I finally ask.

He chokes on a laugh. "What?"

"Your name. Why is it Nik? How are you Nik and also Santa?"

"My name is Nik. Nikolaos. I don't understand your question."

"Where did Santa Claus come from?"

"St. Nikoloas."

"What?"

"Language evolves over time, right? And not only does it evolve, but people get lazy when they talk, and things get misunderstood. So imagine over a thousand years of people saying St. Nikolas. Some people say it faster, other people might not hear them correctly, and over time, with different accents and different people, it evolves."

"Santa Claus is just St. Nikolas?"

He gives me a little closed mouth smile and I can't help but laugh.

"The name Santa Claus is from a thousand-year game of broken telephone?" I ask.

"Give or take. I've actually been referred to as Santa for a much shorter time than anything else. But there were less people in the world when I went by other names, so Santa feels most like my name now. More people use it."

"Yeah, Charlie said something about that," I say, almost under my breath.

Nik just nods as a response.

"But you don't call yourself Santa," I try to confirm. "Like, I don't have to call you Santa."

"No," he says, shaking his head. "I sometimes refer to myself as Santa, depending on the situation. If it calls for it, you know? I know that's what most English-speaking people everywhere else call me. Or, called me. Think they call me. I still don't understand when and why they all stopped believing."

"Me neither. Maybe everyone thought you died. That's what happens to people, after all."

"That's what I thought at first, too. But the elaborate pranks people play, it doesn't make sense to me."

"Pranks?"

"Pretending to be me. Putting out cookies for me but eating them themselves and saying I ate them. Telling children there's a magical elf doll watching them and reporting to me every night, and making their kids believe the doll is moving on its own. Why not fill stockings like I did, maybe have some milk and cookies as a family to honour me, but with no pretending? Why all the lies?"

"I don't know if I would call them lies," I say. "I mean, yeah, I guess they are. But it's just a way to make Christmas fun and magical for their kids."

"It can be fun and magical without all that. I remember seeing the excitement on the faces of the children I delivered presents to before I even had magic. I was just an old man, an old man with nothing magical about me, and I think Christmas was pretty magical back then. Or, it wasn't really Christmas then, not yet, but still, it was basically the same as what Christmas is now. Sort of."

"Are you sure about that?" I ask, hoping he can sense my playful tone.

He grins. "Yes, I'm sure. I'm just trying to say that I saw and even heard the reactions from people when I did this without any magic. And I think it was still magical."

"That's nice," I say. "But I wish you could see Olivia on Christmas morning. I think it would answer your question. What you're describing sounds nice, and I'm sure at the time it was magical. But the way it's done now, I dunno, it's different. It's not just a magical feeling, but like, real magic. And kids only believe in magic for so long, and Christmas is the most magical thing ever as a kid when you think that Santa is real. When you fully believe that a magical man who knows what you want for Christmas is bringing you presents that your parents didn't have to buy. Even the Gingerbread Elf, Olivia is so excited, every morning to find hers."

"Hmm." He seems to be thinking, like he's not totally convinced. "When will you tell her that it's all a rouse?"

I shrug. "Kids usually figure it out on their own. Once they get older, once they start to realize that magic is just something we pretend is real when we're playing games. I don't know."

"That's sad."

"A little."

"Especially because it's not fake. It *is* real. I'm real. I'm very real." He laughs but I have a feeling it's a nervous laughter and he's only doing it to make sure he doesn't cry.

I put my palm against his beard, and he raises his hand, putting it against the back of mine.

"I know you're real," I whisper.

"I wish that was enough."

"Maybe it is." I rub my thumb against his cheek, and he brings his other hand up to the back of my head. I move my thumb towards his mouth, and run it along his bottom lip, and he gently kisses it.

"Do you still like me?" he asks quietly. "Or did I ruin everything?"

"No, I think you fixed everything."

"Really?"

I nod and shift on the couch so that I can swing my leg over his hips and straddle him as I sit on his lap.

"Oh, like I *really* fixed everything," he says.

"Well before I just thought you were delusional. And now I know either you're not, or I am too."

"I promise you're not delusional."

"Okay." I lean my face in closer to his and let myself taste his breath on my lips. "I'm going to kiss you," I whisper.

"Okay."

You would think making out with Santa would be weird. But he doesn't even look like Santa. He looks like a normal guy with a normal beard that's nicely trimmed, wearing normal jeans and a normal hoodie. His hands are normal but *lovely* as they trail up my back under my shirt, and his tongue is normal but also delightful as it finds its way into my mouth. There is nothing weird about any of it, except for the fact that I spent all day exploring the North Pole and interacted with multiple elves, and literally pet Rudolph last night. Oh, and that I teleported here. That's a little weird, I guess, but sitting here, kissing Nik, is not weird. It's amazing.

He shifts us and lays me down on the couch, putting some of his weight on me, which, also normal, but also great. I start to unzip my hoodie and Nik runs his hand up my ribs and then pulls it off my shoulders. I shrug out of it and wrap my arms around his neck, pulling him closer to me. But wait, his hoodie is still on. My fingers find his zipper and I pull it down, and without taking his mouth off mine, he takes it off and tosses it on the floor. I slip my hands under his t-shirt and run my fingers through his chest hair, and I almost start to take his shirt off, but I stop myself. He was the one who said we should go slow, and I also like going slowly, and I was also questioning his sanity just a few days ago, so maybe this is rushing things just a little bit.

"Maybe we should just slow down a little," I whisper. "I kind of got carried away."

"Oh. Sure. Sorry."

We both sit up, and Nik runs his fingers through his hair and straightens it out a little.

"Don't be sorry," I say.

"Is this weird? Because of who I am?"

"No, not at all. Which is kind of weird, when you think about it."

I chuckle and he does too, but my chuckle turns into more of a full laugh, and then I snort, and Nik laughs harder too. I laugh so hard that I'm wheezing and having trouble breathing. I wipe a tear that's fallen and try to calm down, but every time I try to, we just laugh more.

"I just made out with Santa Claus," I cry through my wheezing.

"You're the only one who believes in me," Nik says with the same tone.

"My brother probably thinks I've been kidnapped!"

"You *were* kidnapped!"

"Oh yeah!" I snort again and Nik bursts out even harder from that, and we're both lost again. Lost forever to our laughter.

"So all that stuff you told me about delivering presents to your town, and everyone chipping in, that was all true." We've opened a window to let the crisp air in, and are counteracting the chill by also having a cup of hot chocolate. It's perfect.

"Basically," Nik says. "Except I deliver them all over the world. I just couldn't tell you that part."

"Right, of course. But there's so much you didn't seem to understand. How can you literally *be* Santa Claus, and not know about, say, cell phones, or Apple Pencils? Don't you guys make them for people for Christmas?"

"Yeah, but it's different. We don't know how they work."

"You don't know how they work but you can make them? How?"

Nik shrugs. "Magic. And the only things we've made like that in a really long time are the Apple Pencils, anyway. Oh, and iPads. But that's it. And that was just a desperate idea to get people to believe in me. We used to make things like teddy bears, and yoyos. Blankets, sweaters, blocks, hats, toy boats, and planes. That sort of thing. Stockings were already full from parents long before all these tech things started being a thing."

"Oh shoot."

"Yeah."

"I think you should come back with me," I say.

"Come back with you?"

"Yeah. I think you need to see first hand how much people love Christmas, this version of Christmas, even if they don't think you're real. And how magical it is for kids. We can take Olivia to see Santa at the mall."

"I'm sorry, take her to see me at the mall?"

"Yes. Do you not know about mall Santas?"

"Uh, no, I'm going to say that I don't."

"Oh, weird, I thought you would know about them."

"Why would I know about them? I've known about literally none of the things everyone else does."

"Hmm, okay, you've got a point."

"Wait!" he says, pointing a finger. "Are they like the horrible Santa that was in that movie we watched? That movie where the boy wants a rifle for Christmas?"

"Oh. No." I laugh a little. "It's the same idea, but mall Santas aren't mean like they are in that movie. It's just a way for kids to meet Santa, tell him what they want for Christmas, and get a picture with him."

"Doesn't that ruin the magic?"

"No, I don't think so. I would say it helps it stay alive."

"Is there some sort of schedule?" he asks. "For Santa to visit all the malls? I don't see how anyone would believe that I have time for this."

It's hard for me not to laugh at his response, but I think I do well with a little smirk. "Well they're all different people pretending to be Santa. Every mall gets one, it isn't like, a travelling Santa."

He raises his eyebrows at me and for some reason I feel stupid saying all this out loud. "How is that not ruining the magic?" he asks. "*Every* mall gets a Santa? That's clearly not possible."

"Well we don't tell the kids that there's one in every mall. They just think that Santa is visiting *their* mall, and they don't question anything else about it. Plus it's supposed to be magic, so it doesn't matter, right?"

He shrugs, but gives me a smile. "I suppose. But maybe it is a good idea that I go back with you for a little while."

"Really!?"

"Yeah."

I take the last sip of my hot chocolate and place the mug on the side table. "This is so exciting! And what do I tell my brother? He'll think you kidnapped me for sure."

"If Charlie still can't take us back tomorrow, we might have to go the way I got there."

"How did you get there?"

"Planes. A lot of planes."

"Oh, that sounds awful."

"It wasn't great."

"Don't you have a sleigh? Like, with flying reindeer?"

"I do, yes, but they can only fly on Christmas Eve."

"What?" I feel how high pitched my question comes out and I wince a little.

Nik shrugs. "I don't know, they've only ever been able to fly on Christmas Eve. I've seen them try a couple times throughout the year as if they've forgotten that they can't, or maybe they're just testing it out, and they always fall into the snow. They look around when they get up, like they're making sure no one saw. It's pretty funny, actually, in a sad sort of way."

"Aw, poor things."

"They're okay."

"Well why don't we keep worrying about all that in the morning, then."

"Yeah, that sounds good. I'll let you head to bed."

My heart sinks a little, but I nod and try to make sure my smile doesn't look too forced. "Okay," I say.

"Unless you wanted to sleep in my bed with me?"

"Is that weird?" I ask.

"I don't think so. We just made out on my couch, was that weird?"

"No," I giggle. "It was lovely."

"Well, then let me show you to my room."

Nik's room is amazing. There's a fireplace in here, and a big bookcase double stacked with hardcovers and paperbacks, and besides a few that I saw at the book shop earlier, there are none that I recognize. His bed is probably a King size, with sleigh shaped head and footboards. I run my fingers along the intricate detailing in the wood, snowflakes and swirls that are etched and embossed, with golds and reds running through it all. He pulls the plaid comforter back, revealing deep red sheets that look so silky smooth and soft. I climb onto the mattress and let him get into bed next to me.

I'm about to lie down and curl up when my heart leaps into my throat. "Oh my god!" I screech.

"What?"

"What about Mrs. Claus!?"

"Who?"

"Your wife!" I practically throw myself out of his bed and back up into his dresser. "Oh my god, I'm a homewrecker!"

"What?"

"You're married and I've made out with you! Twice!"

He scrunches his eyebrows at me. "Uh, I'm not married."

"What about Mrs. Claus?"

"You keep saying that. What does that mean?"

"You're Santa Claus, so your wife is Mrs. Claus." I say it slowly though, because I can feel him judging me.

"First of all, my last name isn't Claus, so if I *did* have a wife, she wouldn't be Mrs. Claus, and even if I did, why doesn't she have a first name? Why am I Santa Claus but my wife is just Mrs. Claus?"

"Uh. The Patriarchy?"

"The what?"

I shake my head and take a step towards him. "What's your last name?"

"I don't technically have a last name, but I understand how last names work in the modern world, so I suppose mine would be Myra."

"Huh. You don't understand Apple Pencils but you understand last names."

"To be fair, I understand Apple Pencils *now*. And knowing how last names work is completely different. I know everyone's last names. Knowing what they mean and seeing a clear pattern in them is pretty easy to pick up on."

"Okay," I say slowly. "So. Your last name is Myra, and you don't have a wife."

"I do not have a wife."

"It doesn't make sense to me how much stuff we got wrong when we also got so much right. Like, Rudolph exists for Christ's Sakes, but Mrs. Claus doesn't? How does that even happen?"

"I wish I knew. Because then maybe I could figure the rest of this out before I disappear."

I finally get back into bed and let Nik pull the covers over us both. "I don't think you're going to disappear," I say.

"That's good. I disagree, though."

"Well we'll just have to figure it out together then, won't we?"

"I guess we will."

I move closer to him and rest my head in the corner of his chest where it meets his shoulder. He wraps his arm around me and presses his mouth to the top of my head. I feel like I can't breathe all of a sudden, but it only lasts half a second, and then I'm so relaxed I could melt into his arms.

"This bed is amazing," I say.

"Thanks. I always have the best sleeps in this bed."

"I'm already having trouble keeping my eyes open."

"Good," he whispers. "You need to rest."

Nik

I wake up before Morgan, and I take a minute to admire her. I still can't believe she's here with me. I don't agree with how she got here, but now that she is, and now that she's more comfortable, I'm enjoying it so much. This is my home, the place that I've always felt safe, the place that I didn't even realize I'd missed until I came back. Even when I was throwing up in the snow, and yelling at Charlie, there was this sense of contentment surrounding me, this bubble of safety. I was furious with Charlie and I felt like my head was going to explode, but I was *home*. Where there are no secrets, where everyone knows that I'm real, where I don't have to calculate what I say before I say it. But more than that, where I feel like me. Where the comfort wraps around me like a blanket and fills me with warmth.

Morgan looks so peaceful curled up on her side, her hands tucked under chin. I listen to her breathe for a little while, and it brings me a new comfort I've never felt before. It's so nice that I almost fall back asleep myself. But we need to get going if Charlie is going to take us back today. I boop her nose with my index finger, but she doesn't stir.

"Morgan," I whisper. Her hair is still in its two braids, but some strands have come out near the top and fall across her face.

I gently move them out of the way and then kiss her on the tip of her nose.

She groans but doesn't open her eyes.

"Morgan," I say again, a bit louder this time.

"Mmm," she hums.

"We should get up."

She opens her eyes but somehow sinks deeper into her pillow. "Do we have to?"

"I think it's a good idea."

"Ugghh, fine." But she grabs the blankets and pulls them up to her neck, snuggling deeper into the bed.

"That doesn't look like getting up," I laugh.

"I have a process."

"Oh, a process. Well then, carry on."

She laughs too, a cute little giggle, and one of her hands comes out from under the comforter to gently hit me in the shoulder. "Thanks, I will."

"I'm going to get up. You take all the time you need."

"Okay."

I try not to smile at her, but I can't help it, and I scoot off the bed and pull my side of the blanket up so the bed is partly made. "But don't take too long," I add. "We have to see if Charlie can take you home."

"Oh, right." She throws the covers back and lets out a huge sigh before also getting out of bed. "We have to go talk to the kidnapper."

"Yeah," I say slowly. I'm still upset that Charlie did that, even though I know he misread the situation. "I'm sorry about that," I tell her. "I know it isn't an excuse, and you don't have to forgive him, but he really didn't mean any harm. Things are different up here, and it didn't occur to him. Everyone has good intentions about everything, like, all the time, so he wasn't thinking about it in the same way. I'll admit that I thought he was smarter than that, but he was excited, and he's never done anything like this before."

She shrugs and makes her side of the bed. I wish there was more I could do to make it better. I walk around the bed and put my hands out to her, to do what, I'm not sure, but when she turns around and sees me there, she sort of stops.

"I'm sorry," I say again, quietly.

"I know. But you didn't do anything." She steps closer to me and my hands easily find her hips. She puts her arms around my neck and looks up at me. "It's funny that I was sort of afraid of you kidnapping me, or at least breaking into my apartment to leave presents, and then your friend is the one who did it."

"He knows now that it was kidnapping, but he didn't know that's what he was doing when he did it," I try.

"Yeah," she sighs. "I guess." And then she nods and gives me a little smile.

"But to be fair," I say, "I was totally planning on breaking into your apartment to leave presents."

She stiffens under my touch and pulls back, but doesn't take her arms away from around my neck.

"On Christmas Eve," I clarify. "With magic. Okay, so I wasn't going to *break in;* I was going to appear in your living room through the magic of Christmas and slip a straw or a nice pen, or let's be honest, an Apple Pencil, into your stocking."

She smiles and tilts back a bit, looking up at me with her hands still linked behind my neck. "You know, I got a single, reusable straw in my stocking every year for almost as long as I can remember, but it stopped two Christmases ago."

"Really?"

"Yeah. I loved getting those straws, and it was funny because I obviously didn't get them when I got older and I lived alone and didn't have a stocking anymore. But any time I had a boyfriend and we had stockings together, there was a straw in mine again. And my boyfriends at the time always laughed at the straw because they said they never put them in there."

I can feel myself smiling. "You don't say."

"And I believed them because why would they lie about a silicone straw? But I never really questioned it further. I just thought it was funny."

"And you stopped getting them two years ago? Not- not just last year?"

"Definitely two years ago. And I had a stocking at Brett's the last two Christmases."

"Hmm." I'm not sure what to say. Because while I did stop delivering presents only last year, I didn't add things to every stocking every Christmas. But if I put a straw in Morgan's stocking every year, there's no explanation as to why I didn't give her one two years ago.

"You know what I got two years ago instead?" she asks.

"What?"

She smiles and kisses me on the lips, lingering a little before pulling back and saying, "An Apple Pencil."

"Really?"

"Yeah. It was weird, though, because it wasn't in any packaging, and there's no way anyone I knew would spend that much money on a stocking stuffer. Plus I already had one."

"Oh." I wonder if she can hear the disappointment in my voice.

"But it's nice because if it dies, I have another one I can use right away."

"Oh, that's handy."

"Quite."

We stare at each other for a few long seconds, my hands still on her hips, hers still tangled together behind my neck.

"They were from you, weren't they?" she finally asks.

All I can do is nod.

"That's so cool," she says, and I can hear the smile in her voice.

"You think so?"

"Yes." And she presses her lips to mine again.

She pulls me tighter into her arms and I wrap mine around her back, letting her open her mouth against mine, tasting her tongue. But I slowly pull back, and she looks up at me like she's disappointed.

"Now that you know everything, what do you think about me?" I ask her.

"What do you mean?"

"Do you think that you're actually attracted to me, or do you think it's my magic making you feel that way? Am I… did I take advantage of you?"

She takes in a deep breath as she thinks about her answer, and then she sits on the edge of my bed. I stay standing because I don't want to overstep anymore than I might have already.

"It's hard to say," she starts, "but there's really no way to know. But I do know that when I thought you were a weirdo, I felt different. There was still something tugging at me to give you another chance, but I still had logic, you know? I wanted to give you another chance, but I knew that I shouldn't. I wanted to go back to your apartment, but I didn't. So I don't think that your magic is so strong that it's clouding my judgement or making me do things I don't want to do. Your magic might be a part of it, and it makes sense why I felt so comfortable with you so soon, and I guess that's a little weird when you think about it, but we're both aware of it, right?"

I'm not sure what to say so I just nod.

"I think this will happen to any person you want to pursue a relationship with, and unfortunately, that means there's no real way to know if anyone likes you because of who you are as a person, or because of, um, who you are. And that sucks."

"Yeah."

"And if you're not comfortable pursuing a relationship under those conditions I think that's fair. But I'm aware of it. I have full knowledge of the situation and I still have my logic. I don't think my brain is so clouded with magic that it's making me irrational. I mean I didn't want to be here with you until I met Rudolph."

Is it weird to say that this makes me feel better? "Oh, good," I say. "I was worried about that."

"I still felt safe with you, but I wanted to leave. If that makes sense."

"It does make sense."

"So I think as long as we continue to go slowly, we can keep doing this. I mean, as long as you want to."

"Oh yes, I definitely want to."

She laughs. "Okay, good. Me too."

Charlie lets himself into my house about twenty minutes later, and I'm surprised at how much disappointment I still feel when I look at him.

"Who's ready to go back to Canada!?" he calls as he wanders through my kitchen.

"Hi, Charlie," I say, meeting him by the fridge.

"Where's Morgan?" he asks.

"I'm here." Morgan comes up behind me and I feel the need to wrap an arm around her and comfort her, to make sure she knows that she's safe.

"What's going on?" Charlie asks. "It's tense in here."

"You kidnapped me, Charlie!" Morgan cries.

"Oh, we're still mad about that. Okay." He puts his hands on his hips, but then crosses his arms over his chest. He shakes his head and lets his hands fall to his side, before putting them together in front of his chest. "I'm really sorry," he says to her. "Truly, I am. I promise I'm telling you the truth when I say that I thought you wanted to come here. And when I heard you say you might believe me if I took you to the North Pole, I got so excited. I thought maybe there was actually a way out of this, a way for everyone to believe in my best friend again. My best friend who I've known for the better part of 2000 years was going to disappear into thin air and I thought you were the answer to fixing it! I thought you wanted to see this place and I jumped at the opportunity. I didn't," He stops and licks his lips, and looks away for a second, probably to try and fight back the tears I can see surfacing. "I didn't think it through, and I'm sorry. I just acted. I feel so stupid."

"You made me barf," Morgan says in a clipped tone.

"Okay, and that sucks, but it's not the end of the world, right?"

"It sucked a lot."

"I'm sorry. I'm so sorry. I promise to always think about things before I do them from now on. And to make sure that I have clear and enthusiastic consent from the other participating parties."

"Fine," Morgan says. "I'm glad," she pauses for a second, "that you at least, um, learned from it. And that you'll be more careful in the future. Like," she pauses again, and I want to tell her it's fine, that she doesn't have to be nice to him about this, but she continues. "Like, I get it. I understand what happened. But it was still scary, okay?"

Charlie nods and opens his mouth to say something, but then Morgan quickly asks, "Can you take us back?"

He smiles. "Yes, I believe I can."

Charlie takes Morgan first in case he needs time to rest before doing it again. Then at least Morgan can be home and not be stuck here any longer. It doesn't take long for Charlie to appear back in my living room, coming through a silver-looking portal in the air that he sort of twists out of. It comes with a loud crack and he stumbles when his feet make contact with my floor. He wobbles and grabs a hold of the couch.

"You okay?" I ask.

He nods and holds a hand out. "Your turn."

"Not yet," I tell him.

"What? I'm fine. I can do it one more time."

"No, you're going to rest, so you have enough energy to come back here right away."

"You- you don't want me to stay with you for a bit?" I can hear the quiver in his voice.

"If Morgan is still there, I don't want her to have to see you again."

His eyes get red and glassy, and he nods once. "Um. Okay." His voice cracks and I wince a little.

"It's a lot for her," I try, my voice low.

"Yeah." He nods again and looks away.

"I'm just looking out for her. I think your apology helped, but I can tell she's still a little shaken over it. This whole thing has shaken her, to be honest, and the timing of you taking her didn't help. No matter your reasoning or thought behind it, you still did that to her. And she's allowed to be upset about it."

"Yeah, I know." His tears have finally broken through, and one rolls down his cheek.

"And even though the reason I don't want you to stay is so we can make Morgan feel more comfortable, I do also think that I need to do this without you." I look at him and his face is knitted tightly like he wants to understand but doesn't.

"I want to do it with you," I clarify. "You're my best friend. But I think it's good for me to do this on my own, you know?"

He nods more confidently this time, and wipes the tears from his face. "Okay."

I nod too and let out a deep breath, look around my kitchen. The kitchen that Morgan and I shared meals in. The room right next to the living room, where she felt safe enough with me to let her guard down and be vulnerable. Where even I felt safe enough with her to talk to her more about me and my life. I wonder if any of this will continue.

After I think we've been here long enough to let Morgan get out of my apartment, I look at Charlie again. "Okay," I say. "Let's go."

CHAPTER 20

Charlie deposits me in the living room of my apartment and I immediately look around to see if Morgan is here.

"Morgan!?" I call, heading down the hall to my bedroom. She probably left right away like I had anticipated, but I look around my apartment for her first, just in case. I don't see her in my room, but I do notice that my elf doll has moved. Instead of sitting with my pocket watch on the dresser, he's hanging off the post of my bed's footboard. I smile at it, feeling a little warm and fuzzy inside my chest, and then turn back into the hall.

"She's not here," Charlie says.

"Yeah, she must have gone home."

"Yeah, maybe."

We stand and stare at each other for a few seconds and then I clear my throat.

"I guess I'll go home, too," Charlie says.

I nod. "Sure. See you later."

"Yeah. Are you coming back for Christmas?" he asks. "You need me to pick you up?"

"I probably should, yeah. I mean, just in case."

"Yeah, just in case."

"Okay."

"Okay, yeah," Charlie says.

He starts to turn away but I grab onto his sweater and pull him back, into my chest, and I wrap my arms around him. He hugs me back and sighs.

"We'll get through this," I whisper.

"Sure."

He lets go and steps back, and then disappears into his portal. I am so emotional right now and I don't know how to deal with it. I've been through so much the last few days and it's all starting to hit more than it did as it was happening. It's like now that I'm alone, my thoughts on everything are just smacking me in the head, and it's overwhelming. Charlie took Morgan to the North Pole. *Morgan was in the North Pole. With me.* I introduced her to the reindeer, and showed her around, we ate food together, we *made out*. I was able to share a part of me with someone I never thought I even needed to. A part of me I didn't realize was a secret. And Morgan accepted it all, she accepted *me*. I don't know how to process any of this. How do I make it stop? I go back into my bedroom and then I pace down the hall towards the living room again. I don't know what to do. Maybe I'm hungry. I open the fridge, but just as I open it, I notice that there was a piece of paper on the front. I close the fridge door and stare at the paper stuck to it with a Christmas Tree magnet.

It says *I'm across the hall* in Morgan's loopy handwriting.

I let out a deep breath before knocking on Brett's door. I don't know what I will do if he's the one who answers. But luckily, it's Morgan. She smiles as soon as she sees me, and then steps into the hall and shuts the door behind her.

"Sorry I didn't stay, I just still feel weird around your friend," she says. "I didn't want to see him again. Not yet, anyway."

"I figured."

"My brother isn't here. He's still at my place, I'm sure. Or out looking for me. He's probably reported me missing. I should call him."

"Yes, you should definitely call him."

"I don't know what to tell him."

"Tell him someone tried to kidnap you but I found you and brought you home. That's almost what happened anyway."

"That's so traumatizing."

"Yeah, it was."

"Right. I just don't want him to worry."

"Morgan, he's already worried. It doesn't matter what you tell him. You should call him."

She sighs and nods, and pulls her phone out of her back pocket. "I need to plug it in." She motions for me to follow her into Brett's apartment, so I do, and then shut the door behind me. She finds a cord by the side of the couch in the living room and plugs it in before phoning her brother. I try not to listen, but it's hard not to.

"Hey, I'm okay," she says into the phone. "I'm so sorry I didn't call, time got away from me and I didn't realize you would be worried. Which I know is silly, because you're currently staying at my place because we're worried about someone, but…" I can hear her trying to come up with a reasonable explanation in her tone of voice and I'm worried she's having trouble with it. She waits before speaking again, probably because Brett is saying something. "Um, Nik actually saved me," she continues. "Something happened, and he was there. He helped me." Another pause. "No, I don't really remember much from it. Just Nik being there for me." I lean on the wall behind me and cross my arms. "We're at your place right now. I'm sure Nik can take me home. Okay, see you soon."

"I can drive you," I say.

"Thank you."

I walk Morgan up to her apartment and her brother practically tackles her in the doorway. He's crying, and so then she starts to cry, and I'm standing in the corridor not sure what to do with myself. When they finally pull away from each other, Brett looks at me, and then steps across the floor to me and pulls me in for a hug as well.

"Thank you for being there," he whispers.

"Of course. I'm just glad she's okay."

"Me too."

"I'll let you two catch up. Make sure you're both okay," I say.

"Oh, you don't have to leave," Morgan tells me.

"It's okay, I think I need to be alone for a bit anyway. I'm uh, I'm glad everything's okay."

"Okay. Thank you."

"Of course."

I start to go back toward the elevator when Morgan calls after me. "Wait," she says, "I still haven't given you my phone number."

"Oh."

"I'm assuming you don't have your phone on you right now?"

"No, I don't."

"If I give you my number on a piece of paper, will you know how to text me?"

I can't help but smile. "I'm sure I can figure it out."

"Okay." She runs into her apartment and comes back out with a little folded piece of paper. I take it and keep it gripped in my hand the entire way home.

I give Morgan as much space as I can. I'm not sure what details she's going to tell her brother, but I'm sure she's not going to tell him that she was taken to the North Pole and that she met Rudolph. I hope he doesn't ask me about it the next time I see him. Which might be any time, seeing as he lives across the hall from me.

After two days, I decide to get my phone working and send a message to Morgan. Opening the messaging app and putting her number into the recipient line is easy enough, and there's a keyboard laid out right on the screen, so I tap my thumbs on the letters I need to write her a message.

Hi Morgan. I hope you're doing well. What did you tell Brett? Do I need to have a story ready for the next time I see him? Is he still staying with you for a while? Also I saw that my elf moved. It made me smile.

You don't need to have a story for Brett comes her reply. **I told him it wasn't a big deal, I just said that I slipped on some**

ice and hit my head, but that you were there and brought me to the hospital and everything was fine.

But what if he asks anyway?

He won't, it's not like he thinks I'm lying. I said I hadn't contacted him because I was distracted by the whole thing, and then by you, and I didn't know my phone died. I don't want to worry him any more than he already has been she sends.

Okay, that makes sense I reply.

I also told him that you don't think you're Santa Claus. That I misunderstood you.

Oh good I type back to her.

Do you want to come skating with us tomorrow night?

I would love to.

I drive over to the park myself and meet them for skating. I don't have any skates, but luckily there's a hut with someone renting them out. I get a pair of stiff, black skates with white laces, and I'm just finishing tying them up when Morgan, Olivia, and Brett come waddling up to me, all in their skates already.

"Hey," Morgan says.

I smile and say hi back, but I really want to kiss her. Instead I let her and her family lead me through the snow and onto the skate trail that goes all through the park, around trees, and through what looks like an old, abandoned village. It loops around old log cabins and past benches with families taking breaks. Lights are strung up on either side of the trail, creating a glowing barrier that illuminates the ice, making it look like it and everything on it is glowing. Morgan grabs onto my hand and we skate side-by-side, watching Brett and Olivia skate ahead of us.

"This is really cool," I say. "I like this better than a rink."

"Do you have a rink at home? I never saw one."

"Yes, we have a few. But no one has thought of having a trail. It's a great idea. I'll have to bring it back to everyone. I'm sure they would love it."

"They definitely would."

A little girl skates up to me and grabs my other mittened hand. "Are you Santa?" she asks.

I smile and look down at her, giving her hand a gentle squeeze. "What would you say if I told you I was?"

She gasps and stops skating, so I do as well.

"Do you want to tell me what you want for Christmas?" But I already know. She wants a-

"I want a pink Instax camera," she says.

"That's a great gift idea. Thank you for sharing that with me, Carly."

She gasps again, and smiles.

"I'll do my very best to make sure you get a pink Instax camera, okay?" I say.

She smiles and then skates off.

"Whoa," Morgan says.

"What?"

"That girl just knew who you were."

I shrug, and start skating again. "Yeah, a lot of kids do."

"That's why Olivia said you looked like Santa."

I chuckle at that. "Poor Olivia must be confused. The first time I met her, her dad was threatening to phone me and tell me that she'd been misbehaving."

"Oh, dear god."

I don't know what else to say, but I do laugh again. "It's been really nice, having kids know me. It's been a long time since I've experienced it. Like, a *long* time."

"How do you do it? Are you going to bring her a camera?"

"I'm sure her parents already got her one. They always do."

"What if they got her the wrong colour?"

"I don't know. She'll have a camera in a colour she didn't want."

"And then she'll stop believing in you."

"But you said everyone stops."

"Yeah, but now that I know you're real, I want to help you. You have to bring her a pink Instax camera."

"Okay."

She smiles and tugs on my arm. "Come on. Let's catch up."

It starts to snow, and the big flakes land on the lights along the trail and on the ice in front of us, and our skates cut through it easily. It was a bit louder earlier, with families here together, laughing and talking, but I guess it's getting late, and the trail has quieted down. Our blades slice and whoosh through the sounds of the occasional person walking alongside the trail, the snow crunching under their boots. When we get closer to Brett and Olivia near the end of the trail loop, I can hear laughing. It brings me so much joy to hear Olivia laugh, and I want to catch up to them faster.

Once we're all together again, Brett buys us all hot chocolate. We use the cups to keep our fingers warm, and stand in a circle blowing on our drinks and taking occasional sips.

It's a perfect evening.

The evening is made even more perfect when Morgan suggests that Brett and Olivia head back to their home, and Morgan and I go to her place. I see Brett whispering to her, probably making sure that she's okay, but I also see her nodding, and shoving him a little, I'm sure telling him that she's fine. We wave goodbye in the parking lot after I've brought my skates back and Morgan has changed into her boots. I carry her skates for her to my rental car, and she smiles at me once we're both inside.

"Thanks for coming," she says. "I had a really fun time."

"Yeah, so did I. It was great."

"Excellent. So do you want to go back to my place and watch a Christmas movie?"

"Yeah, that sounds lovely."

We hold hands in the elevator and I can't help but feel giddy inside. She leads me down the corridor and we take our boots off outside her door so we don't track snow into her apartment. Morgan makes us popcorn in her microwave, and we put on a DVD called *We're No Angels*.

"This is my and my dad's favourite," Morgan tells me as she plugs in her Christmas tree. She turns the main living room light off before sitting on the couch, and the colourful lights on the tree glow in warm circles.

"Oh, that's nice."

"We try to watch it together every year."

"But you're watching it without him," I say.

"Oh, it's okay, I'll watch it again."

I can tell the movie is quite a bit older than all the ones I watched with Charlie. The film quality and the colour are quite degraded, and the sound is a little weird, but the movie itself is fantastic. There are so many things that I don't understand, but a lot that I put together with context clues, and I laugh out loud more than a few times. Santa doesn't show up in this story; but it's not needed. It's not about 'real' magic, it's more about the magic of family, and kindness, and a little colourful snake who is apparently very deadly.

"Do your elves know how to make Instax Cameras?" Morgan asks me when the movie's over. She's grabbing our cups and popcorn bowls, so I get up and follow her to the kitchen.

"I'm sure they can figure it out," I say.

"Do you even know what an Instax camera is?"

"A type of camera. That comes in different colours."

"But how can you make these presents for kids if you haven't even heard of them before?" She puts our dishes in the sink and then turns around to face me, leaning on the counter behind her.

"I don't know, but we can. We haven't made cameras, but we made Apple Pencils, and those work, don't they?"

"Yeah. I just don't understand how you even know what kids want. There's no way you're getting their letters."

"Letters?" I ask. "They send me letters?"

Morgan laughs. "Yes! But they go to volunteers and-" she cuts herself off and looks to the side for a second, scrunching her whole face like she's thinking. "Actually, I have no idea where they go and who answers them. But it's definitely done by different people depending on where you live."

"What's done by different people?"

"They reply to all the letters."

"As me?"

"Yes!"

"Are there very few children who write me letters?"

"No, almost every kid does it."

"Well it's clearly impossible for one man to reply to all those letters."

"Obviously, that's why volunteers do it. Or whoever does it."

"Why does everyone always think I have all this time on my hands?"

"Nik. You deliver presents all over the world in one night, I don't think people are concerned with how long it takes you to do something."

"But I can only deliver presents to everyone in one night because time moves so slowly when I do it. It practically stands still."

"Right, yeah, you told me that. But people don't know that's how it works, and I guess they figure if you can magic your way through that, you can do it with anything. Also according to everyone else in the world, you're not real. You're just a story they tell to their kids, so it doesn't matter if you have time to do it or not."

"Right. Well we can make things even if we don't understand them. We haven't made anything that complex, because like I said before, we mostly stopped making things a long time ago, but I'm confident we can make these cameras."

"Okay, but how do you know what everyone wants if you don't get their letters?"

I shrug. "I just do. Most kids want the same thing as each other every year anyway, and all the different ones find their way through."

"Find their way through?"

"To me."

"But what do you mean?"

"I don't know! I just know what everyone wants and I tell the workshop elves what to make. And when I get to each house, I reach into my bag, and the right present comes out. It just happens. Did you really used to think I sat at home reading millions of letters?"

"No," she says slowly, crossing her arms.

"You thought I read everyone's letters."

"No, I didn't," she says, but she's having trouble hiding a huge smile.

"This is fun," I laugh, and she shoves me in the shoulder.

"It's not my fault!" she shouts playfully.

"Well it's someone's fault."

"Yeah, my parents' fault for lying to me as a kid!"

"You're cute," I say.

"Oh. Not as cute as you."

I smile at her and she takes a step closer to me, allowing me to wrap an arm around her waist. She looks up at me and brings her lips to mine. But she only kisses me for a couple seconds and then pulls back.

"So, when this is all over, are you going to look like Classic Santa? Do you just look like this for undercover purposes?"

"I do look like this for undercover purposes, but it's my understanding that I'm not going to change back to how I looked before, when this is over. I mean, I will eventually, over time. But it'll take a few years."

"Just a few?"

"Sorry, not a few," I say. "More like thirty or forty years. It's my understanding that I'll age at a normal rate and then slow down again once I get back to where I was before I went undercover."

"So if you were to live here or something, like, hypothetically, or if we just stayed together for a little bit of time, we would technically age together?"

"I believe so, yes."

"Not that I want to marry you or anything, I mean this hasn't," she stops and swallows, I assume trying to backtrack, "I mean, I haven't been," she stops again and lets out a shaky laugh. "I know we haven't been together for long, or I mean, we aren't even together, like we haven't even talked about it, but we have kissed a few times, and slept in the same bed, and besides the fact that you live very far away from me, I don't see a reason to just stop doing this unless there's a real incompatibility, right? Like I would like to see where this goes, but I just didn't want to put time into it if you were going to turn into a 75-year-old man on Christmas Eve."

"I know exactly what you're saying. And I feel the same."

"Really?"

"Yes. And even though we live very far away from each other, we can easily visit since I know someone who can teleport and take people with him."

"Oh right, yes, that is quite convenient."

"Very."

"The throwing up part isn't, though," she adds.

"No. But it would be worth it to see you."

We are taking Olivia to see Santa. At the mall. I'm not sure why, but I'm nervous. I'm nervous to see what it's like, and what this Mall Santa is like. Is his image going to be what most other people see when they think of me? And okay, I know that adults don't think I'm real, but they still talk about me like I am. They have Mall Santas, and they have movies about Santa, and their Santa replies to letters that their children write. And while I know I am none of these Santas, in a way, I am. The way people perceive me is the realest it's felt ever since I found out about adults thinking I'm fake.

Is that weird?

"Are you coming?" Morgan asks, pulling me from my thoughts.

"What? Sorry. Yes." I clear my throat and pick up the pace so I can catch up. Brett and Olivia are ahead of us passing stores with sparkling displays, and we trail behind a little, watching them as Olivia skips with joy, her little hand holding on tightly to Brett's.

"Are you okay?" Morgan asks.

"Sorry, yeah. I think."

"This is weird, isn't it?"

"No. No, of course not."

"It's weird. But I thought this would be good for you to see. So you can see how excited all the kids are about it. Even the parents get excited."

We pass a store with a display of Christmas pyjamas in the window, and I want to go in and look around. "Why are the parents excited?" I ask.

"Because their kids are. It's like we're experiencing magic by watching them experience it."

I slow down as I turn the corner and see a wooden house with red trim, fake Christmas trees dusted with something to look like snow, and a path lined with fluffy cotton which I'm assuming is supposed to be snow, leading around the other side of the house. There are families lined up nicely along the path, talking quietly and smiling as they wait their turn. We get in line behind Olivia and Brett and they both turn and smile at us when we arrive.

"What are you going to ask Santa for?" Morgan asks Olivia.

"Wait, can I guess?" I say.

"Yeah!" Olivia smiles and practically jumps up, she's so excited.

"You're going to ask for an iPhone."

"How did you know!?"

"Livvy, you can't ask Santa for an iPhone," Brett says gently.

"Why not?" she asks.

"Because you're too young for a cell phone. If you ask him to get you one, he'll feel really bad not fulfilling your wish."

"But Santa has to get you what you ask for!"

"No he doesn't, Livvy," Morgan says. "Santa takes into account what the parents are comfortable with."

He does?

"He does?" Olivia asks.

"Yup. Didn't I tell you about the year I asked Santa for a trampoline?"

Olivia shakes her head.

"Well," Morgan starts again, "I really wanted a trampoline. Not one of those big backyard ones, just a single-person-jump-on-the-spot trampoline. But my mom, your Grammie, didn't want me to have one because they're loud. I think that was the reason, anyway. But anyway, so Santa didn't get me a trampoline."

Olivia gasps. "He didn't!?"

Morgan shakes her head. "No, he got me a Hop 55. One of those big bouncy balls with a handle that you sit on and bounce around the house with. But he also wrote me a letter apologizing for not getting me the trampoline, but that he couldn't in good conscience get me something he knew my mom wouldn't approve of."

"Santa really wrote you a letter?"

"Yeah! He didn't want me to be too disappointed."

"Did you like it? The Hop ball thing?"

"Yes! I loved it!"

"Oh! That's good! But I really want an iPhone."

"You're not getting an iPhone," Brett says.

She starts to cry, but not like the way she was crying when we first met. It's a little sniffle and a whine, a shake in her voice as she talks. "But I really want one."

"I know you do, sweetie. But who are you going to call on it, anyway?"

"Auntie Morgan!"

"You see Auntie Morgan almost every day, and you already call her on my phone."

"But I want my own."

Brett kneels down so that he's at eye level with his daughter, and grabs onto her hands. "Olivia, this is not the place to do this. Do you really want all these kids to see you crying because you're not getting a phone for Christmas? Do you want Santa to see you like this?"

"N-no," she cries.

"Listen," he says gently. "You're allowed to be upset about this, okay? I would be upset too if I wasn't getting something I really wanted. But I promise you will appreciate a phone much more when you're older. And there's gotta be other things you want for Christmas."

"Yeah," she says.

"What else do you want?"

"An Instax camera. A yellow one."
"Hey, that's a good idea! What else do you want?"
She shrugs and doesn't say anything.
"Slime?" Brett suggests.
"Yeah, I love slime." She smiles and it looks genuine.
"There we go. So why don't you ask Santa for that camera? And some slime for your stocking."
"Okay."
Brett stands up again but he's still got a hold of one of her hands. She leans into him as we continue to wait in line and I can't help but smile at them.

When it's our turn for Olivia to see Santa, I decide to start paying attention. I wasn't watching the other kids talk to Santa because I wanted to experience it for the first time with someone I sort of knew. I didn't want any spoilers, if you will.

His suit is bright red and very clean looking, like it was just made and he's wearing it for the first time. It also doesn't look very warm. His beard is clearly fake, and it looks like some of the strands from it are getting in his mouth. Olivia starts to walk up to him and he leans back and says "ho ho ho" in a deep, jolly sort of laugh. Is this a thing that people think I do?

"What's your name, dear?" he asks her, which is the first mistake. I know everyone's names. But I suppose people who aren't magic would have no way of just knowing the name of every person who comes to see them, so not giving the fake Santa that ability was probably a smart choice.

"Olivia," she says quietly.

"Oh, it's so nice to meet you, Olivia! Would you like to come sit on my lap and tell me what you want for Christmas?"

Olivia nods her head and then Brett steps forward and helps her onto the Mall Santa's lap.

"So, Olivia, have you been a good girl this year?" he asks her.

She shrugs. "I tried to be."

"That's all that we can ask of a child, isn't it Olivia!" He laughs and Olivia smiles. "I'm glad you've tried to be good. Now tell me, what would you like for Christmas?"

"A yellow Instax camera."

"Is yellow your favourite colour?"

She smiles and nods.

"Then I will try my very best to get you a yellow Instax camera."

"Okay."

"Are we doing a picture?" A woman I hadn't noticed before asks. She's standing to the side and she has on a bright green and red outfit, and a long hat with a bell on the end.

"Yes please," Brett says.

Mall Santa and Olivia pose and smile for the photographer who snaps two pictures. A bright flash goes off each time, and then Olivia hops off his lap and walks through the little white gate leading everyone away.

"That was nice, wasn't it?" Brett asks Olivia after paying and getting a print out of the photo.

"I guess. But I don't think that was actually Santa."

"What makes you say that?" Brett asks, taking her hand.

"Jenny White at school said that the people at the mall are just pretending to be Santa."

"And you believe her?" Morgan asks.

"I don't know."

"What if the people at the mall *were* just pretending?" I ask. "That doesn't mean Santa isn't real. It just means the Santas at the mall aren't."

"What's the point in telling him what I want for Christmas if it isn't really him?"

"Well," I start, coming up with a fake explanation on the spot, but feeling pretty good about it. "I think a lot of people can have a hard time believing that you don't actually need to tell Santa what you want for Christmas."

She looks up at me and scrunches her eyebrows. "What do you mean?"

"Santa knows what everyone wants for Christmas. He doesn't need the kids to tell him."

"He doesn't?"

"No! But telling kids that he just knows with magic might be hard to believe, right? How can Santa just *know* what every kid in the world wants for Christmas?"

"How *does* he know?"

"I don't know, that's the thing. He just knows. It's magic. And sometimes magic needs a little help to get people to believe in it. So Santa hires people to pretend to be him and go to malls, so kids can be a part of it, and it can feel more real."

"Santa hires them!?"

"Of course he does!" I say with a smile. Coming up with this explanation for Olivia is actually really fun, and seeing the excitement come back in her face is making me all warm inside. I might be starting to understand why parents do this. "You didn't think the mall people hired them, did you?"

"Sort of."

"Well they don't. Santa does."

"Does Santa really look like that?"

"I guess he does in a way."

"I think he looks more like you."

"Do you?"

"Yeah."

"Well that's a very nice compliment."

She smiles, and I look over at Brett, who mouths 'thank you' at me. I smile and nod, and we head to the car.

CHAPTER 23

Morgan and I head to her gallery so that I can pick up my artwork I bought from her. I want to find somewhere to hang it in my apartment, but I want more to bring it back to the North Pole with me and find a place for it in my house. I would love for Morgan to come with me, to help me pick out the perfect spot, but I'm afraid that she won't want to come with me. I'm afraid that if I ask her, she'll instead ask me to stay here forever, and never go back to my home.

We find a spot to hang the warrior mouse in my living room, and we stand back admiring it for a few minutes. Her hand finds mine and I let her link our fingers together. I sigh when she leans her head on my shoulder; it feels amazing.

"Are you going to go back to the North Pole?" she asks.

"Yes," I whisper.

"When?"

"When I'm done delivering presents on Christmas Eve."

"But you'll come back here, right?"

"I can't keep this apartment. We aren't using real money to pay for it, and my credit card isn't even real. We've basically been stealing this whole time, and I would like to stop that as soon as possible."

"You mean you've been naughty?" she says in a playful tone.

"I suppose. But that's not a thing that I care about," I say with a shrug. "Never has been."

"Oh."

"All kids are good."

"I guess."

"Sorry to disappoint." I chuckle and kiss the top of her head. "What should we do today?"

"Well, I need to do some Christmas shopping. Do you want to join me?"

"I would love that."

Morgan and I spend the next two weeks going shopping, eating at restaurants, and watching Christmas movies. I learn a lot more about what the world – or at least Canada – thinks of me and how I'm perceived, and what different families do to celebrate me and Christmas. We eat at the fancy pizza place again, Carter's, and at the brewery as well, and I find out people call it Friendly's for short, which I very much enjoy. They have two new beers out and I admire Morgan's artwork on the cans. We sip Christmas themed hot drinks on the couch of the coffee shop, and walk hand in hand along the path that takes us around the now-frozen bay. The trees are covered in fluffy snow, and when it comes down in big flakes around us, I have to stop and catch my breath. It's so beautiful that I almost can't believe it's real.

"So I know we keep tiptoeing around the subject," I say on the evening of the twenty-third, "but we need to talk about it."

Morgan lets out a breath and it makes a cloud in front of her face.

"I'm going to go back to the North Pole tomorrow night. And I would love it if you came with me."

"Wait, what?"

"You don't have to, and if you would rather, I can visit you throughout the year and we can decide what you want to do next year."

"You want me to come back with you? Like, to live with you?" I'm afraid to say the words out loud so instead I just nod.

"Wow. Um. Okay."

I hold a mittened hand out to her but she doesn't take it. "Are you okay?" I ask.

"Yeah. I'll be okay. Um. I don't know. Like we haven't been together for very long; if you were a normal person, there's no way we would even be thinking about discussing moving in together."

"You're right," I say. "But we don't have to live together."

"How would I move to the North Pole with you if we aren't living together?"

"You can have your own house."

"I can't pay for a house, Nik."

"We don't pay for things there, remember?"

"People are just going to build me a house for free?"

"Yes. I told you, the Elves love what they do, and they do it because it brings them joy. Not all the Elves build houses, Morgan. Just the ones who love to build houses. Just like not every Elf has their own coffee shop, and not every Elf is an author, or a musician. And you can contribute as well by providing artwork for people to display in their houses or businesses. You can come back with me and still have your own place, for as long as you want."

"That's... an idea," she says slowly. "But I honestly don't know if I can live there all year. Like, I love Christmas, and the snow and everything, and all the magic and stuff, but all year? And away from my family? I have a job here, Nik. Your job is only one night a year, and you probably don't even have to do it, so why can't you stay here?"

"I told you I can't keep my apartment. It's not right."

"What if you stayed at my place?"

"But I thought you didn't want to move in together?"

"I said if you were a normal person we wouldn't be discussing this yet."

I stand up a little straighter, I think understanding what she means. "But I'm not a normal person," I say.

"Exactly."

"I think we should probably be treating it like I am. Just because I'm magic doesn't mean we should rush things."

"Yeah, I guess."

I look around at the downtown stores around us, colourful twinkle lights lining their windows, and then turn back to her. "Plus the North Pole is my home. I can't imagine being away from it any longer than I already have. I've lived there for almost 2000 years, Morgan."

"Right, so don't you want to make a change?"

I laugh a little. "One might think."

"Why don't we take the year to think about it, then? Visit each other. And decide next Christmas."

"Yeah. That sounds good."

"Okay." She presses into my side and together we walk towards the water.

"Are you going to come over for Christmas Eve tomorrow?" she asks. "Hang out with me and Brett and Olivia? My parents will be there too, but they usually leave early."

"I can't, I'll be gone Christmas eve."

"Like even at supper time?"

"Yeah, the other side of the world starts Christmas before we do over here!"

"Oh yeah, I forgot about that."

"But I might be able to come by for a little bit. In the morning?"

"Sounds perfect."

We spend the rest of the evening at my apartment, since it won't be my apartment anymore after tonight. She brings over the last of her Christmas presents, and I help her wrap them as we sit on the floor and watch a movie called *Die Hard.*

Morgan moves my elf doll while I'm in the washroom, and I smile when I find him hanging from the top of my Christmas Tree. I immediately wrap my arms around Morgan and she kisses me, slow and deep. I run my fingers through her hair, which is out of its braids today, and her hands find their way under my hoodie. I let her unzip it and slide it off my shoulders, and then I pull her sweatshirt off over her head. We haven't done a lot of undressing over these past few weeks, and I'm glad how slow we've taken it. I've had time to get to know her more, to know that I'm comfortable with her and she is with me, instead of it just being because of magic. I lay her down on the couch and she curls a leg around me, pulling me closer to her. I let her hands explore my body and I run my fingers up her ribcage, and all I can think about is how I came here to try and find out why people don't believe in me, and instead I found her. I came in search of answers and instead of getting any, I fell in love.

Morgan and I have been lying in her bed since the sun coming through the windows woke us up early this morning. We left my apartment late last night, so we wouldn't be there when Charlie arrived to take care of all the stuff. He said he could take most of it back to the North Pole with him, and anything he couldn't take, he would give it away on something he recently discovered called Kijiji. I wanted to give Morgan her space from Charlie so she can feel comfortable with him on her own timetable, if even at all, so we left by midnight to sleep at her place. And we're still here.

"You know, I've been thinking," Morgan says as she rolls over to face me.

"Oh yeah? About what?"

"Why you haven't disappeared even though no one has believed in you in hundreds of years."

"Why?"

"It's the parents."

I sit up in bed. "What do you mean?"

She sits up too and puts her hand against my cheek, her thumb rubbing against my beard. "The parents have been keeping the magic of Christmas alive this whole time. They do so much to make it magical for their kids, and to make their kids believe that magic even exists. They wait until they're asleep to move dolls and make it look like they're getting into trouble, they fill their stockings and eat the cookies their kids leave out, but make sure to leave some behind so it looks like Santa was in a rush. They decorate their houses, and bake Christmas themed cookies, some parents even dress up like Santa so their kids can catch them in the act! Or they go on the roof so it sounds like the reindeer are up there. It doesn't matter if adults think you're fake. Their kids don't. And it's because of all these adults that kids believe. Children's parents have been keeping you alive since the 1800's."

"I never thought of that."

"So you're not going to disappear." She smiles and runs her thumb over my bottom lip, so I kiss it. I lean in and kiss her lips, letting her take my breath away.

"I'm not going to disappear," I whisper.

Brett's apartment is decorated more heavily than it was the last time I came by, and I'm delighted to see a decorated garland over the doorway and colourful twinkle lights around the big windows in his living room and kitchen. His apartment smells warm and sweet, and it makes me feel so relaxed and welcome. Olivia runs down the hall to greet us when we step inside and she practically squeals in delight.

"Guess what!" she says. "Daddy said I can open one present before I go to bed!"

"Which one are you going to choose?" Morgan asks.

"Dad has to pick it, he said."

"It's pyjamas," Morgan whispers, leaning into my ear.

"Thanks for coming," Brett says, pulling a sheet of cookies out of the oven. "I still have to set up the food trays before my parents get here, but they're not coming until later. I'm sorry you'll probably miss them."

I wave him off. "No worries. I'm just happy I was able to come at all. Can I help with anything?"

"Actually, that would be great."

Brett turns on a video of a fireplace on his TV and plays soft music with bells and people singing, that I have come to recognize as Christmas music. It's so interesting how some traditions from me and the North Pole have continued all these years, but most of them are things I've never heard of. The music is nice. I'm going to play it for everyone when I get back home.

Brett and I make trays of crackers, meats, cheeses, and fruit, while Olivia and Morgan play with toys together in the living room. I can hear them laughing over the sound of the music sometimes and it makes me smile. When the trays are done, we bring them to the coffee table, and then Olivia gets up and brings some of the cookies over, finding a place for them next to the cheese.

"You can help yourself; we don't need to wait for my parents to get here before we eat. There's so much of it," Brett says. So I grab a napkin and put some snacks onto it, before sitting back on the couch to watch one of Olivia's favourite Christmas movies, which is 'really old' according to her, and about someone who takes over being Santa because the last one fell off a roof.

It's funny that even in movies when Santa is supposed to be real, the parents don't believe in him. I haven't related to something so much in quite a while.

I leave Brett's well before their parents are supposed to arrive, and Morgan comes into the hall to say goodbye to me.

"Let them use their same wrapping paper for presents that are from you," she whispers to me. "Let them do your job for you. They like doing it, I promise. Even if they say they don't, the looks on their kids' faces in the morning makes it all worth it. But you can still do your job too. Keep sliding straws or whatever else fits into their stockings. Eat some of the treats. Leave an extra present, even if the parents already bought them. Parents pretending to be Santa makes them and their kids happy. But if just being yourself makes you happy, keep doing it."

I smile at her. "Okay. I will."

"And please bring Olivia a yellow Instax. Brett couldn't find a yellow one anywhere, and he had to get her a pink one. I told him not to worry about it, but of course I couldn't tell him why."

"Is he planning on writing a letter from me about it?"

"He was going to, but I convinced him it wasn't necessary."

My grin gets wider. "Maybe I can write a letter. Explaining why she also has a pink one."

"That would be great."

"I'll come by your apartment later, but you won't know," I say. "It'll be so fast for you, you won't even notice."

"Well I look forward to it anyway."

I smile and give her hand a little squeeze before stepping across the hall to my apartment.

"I'll visit you soon," I say.

She nods, and watches me go inside. I let out a deep breath and stare at my empty apartment, at the bare walls, at the circles in the carpet where the couch used to be. I step into the kitchen to find my elf doll sitting on the counter, leaning against the backsplash. Charlie must have decided I wanted to keep it. Which I did. I smile and pick him up, admiring all the things about him that I thought were creepy when I first got him. He really is quite charming. His brown outfit with colourful trimmings and floppy hat looks like someone decorated him on a cozy snowy day. I hear Brett's door open and close across the corridor and I know that Morgan has gone back to join her family. I'm not really sure why, but I start to cry.

"Merry Christmas!" Charlie shouts as he appears on the other side of my kitchen. "Oh. What's wrong?"

I shrug and wipe the tears from my face. "I don't know. I've never felt this way before."

"Felt what way?"

"I don't know!" I cry. "I'm going to miss it here. And miss Morgan. But I'm excited to deliver presents. It feels more magical to me this year than it has since I can remember. I haven't even started yet, but knowing how much effort parents put in to make this day magical for their kids is making me so happy. They think I'm fake but they try so hard to make their kids believe I'm not, because it's *fun*. Because it makes something impossible seem real."

"But it's not impossible."

"Yeah, *we* know that, and now Morgan does too, but no one else does! I was lost somewhere along the way. People probably did think that I died, which makes sense, because that's what happens to people, and over the years the stories about me and the traditions around it evolved. Like my name. Like people didn't want to just continue my traditions, they wanted to keep me alive somehow. By pretending to be me."

"Ooohh, yeahh!" Charlie points a finger at me in excitement. "You're right! Why didn't we come to this conclusion before?"

"We didn't understand before. I didn't understand. I needed to come here, to be shown all of this, in order for it all to make sense."

"Well I'm glad I came up with this idea, then!"

"Yeah," I say, thinking of Morgan, "so am I."

Charlie takes me back to the North Pole and helps me set up the sleigh. He makes sure I have a thermos of hot chocolate, and all the Elves gather around the town centre to see me off. Rudolph leads the reindeer and after everyone does their countdown, they start running. Almost immediately, we rise into the air and I lean over the sleigh to wave to everyone down on the ground. They jump and cheer for me, and I listen to their joyous shouts until we're so far into the distance that I can't hear them anymore. We fly even farther and the lights of our town get smaller until I can't see them anymore either. The cold wind whips at my face and I close my eyes, take a deep breath, and revel in it.

I find myself smiling with every long skinny object I slide into stockings, and I do a little tap dance on my toes with the first present I put under a tree. I'm pretty sure this present has already been purchased for this child, but I give it to them anyway. It feels exhilarating.

I eat cookie remnants and bring pieces of carrots to the reindeer. But as I pick some up that have been half eaten, I notice the plate they're on. It has three reindeer on it, one of them with a glowing red nose. The words *Reindeer need snacks too* is across the top in child-like writing, and I chuckle. Have parents been taking bites out of carrots and leaving the remnants in the house for their children to find in the morning as if the reindeer came into the house to eat them? Or did they think I brought the leftovers back in case they wanted a healthy snack with dried slobber on it? I shake my head as I put them in my coat pocket. Some of this pretending stuff has clearly not been thought through properly. But the thing that made me realize everyone was pretending to be me was the fact that they used the same wrapping paper, so I suppose I shouldn't be surprised.

After thousands of houses and not finding even a partial or pretend-half-eaten apple for Rudolph, I take it upon myself to go to someone's fridge and find one myself. They have a few royal gala and a golden delicious. I take the royal gala and put it in my pocket before finding a pad of paper on their fridge door and tearing a piece off it. I open and close a few drawers before I find a red pen, so I take the cap off and write them a note.

I took an apple for Rudolph, I hope that's okay. They're her favourite and I'm not sure people know that. – S

I write my next letter under Brett and Olivia's Christmas Tree. Her pink Instax camera is poking out of her stocking, and I stare at it as I think of how to start my letter to her. I'm not sure how I want to word it, but I know I have time to think about it, so I sit in their chair and bask in the glow of the colourful lights. I tap the pen on the arm rest a few times, and then tap it on my mouth, trying to come up with the perfect words. I'm not sure I do, but I think of the story that Morgan told Olivia about the trampoline, and something comes to me.

Hi Olivia. I am so glad that I got to meet you this year. I'm so sorry that your instax camera isn't yellow. But I went through something big this year, and I wasn't as prepared as I normally am for Christmas. So parents said they would help me out this year and buy some of the presents. Your dad was so generous and said that he would get your camera for me. But all the stores were sold out of yellow ones. He tried so hard to get you the colour that you wanted. And sometimes it isn't the presents that we receive that are important, but the thought that goes into them. Your dad loves you very much, and he put so much effort in to get you your camera. If you still want a yellow one by next year, I can bring you one then.

I read the letter over a couple times before I sigh and tear it up into little pieces. It doesn't feel right. It's too forced, feels like something someone would say in one of those Christmas movies. I cross the living room into the kitchen and toss all the little pieces into the garbage, watching them float down to make sure they all make it in the bin. Then I grab a new piece of paper, write a new note, and stick it to a yellow Instax camera, before placing it under her stocking.

The elves accidentally made too many cameras. So you get a yellow one and *a pink one! Merry Christmas! – S*

For some reason I feel the need to be quiet while I'm in Morgan's apartment. I'm afraid that I'm going to wake her up accidentally, even though I know I literally can't. I tiptoe through her living room and plug in her Christmas tree, because she didn't for some reason. She has an empty stocking hanging off her TV stand, and I chuckle. She left it for me to fill. I go into my bag and pull out all the things I know she wants. Her favourite face mask, colourful hair ties, fuzzy socks, a new toque, nail polish, a Terry's

Chocolate Orange. Mini eggs, Ferrero Roché, and just for some laughs, a big handful of reusable straws.

I jump at the creek of a door opening, and turn to see Morgan standing in the hallway.

"Nik?" she asks.

"Morgan?"

"Hi." She smiles and pads down the hall towards me.

"How are you doing that?" I ask.

"Doing what?"

"This."

"I'm not doing anything."

"You're in my time bubble," I say.

"Your time bubble?"

"Yeah, time moves slower for me on Christmas Eve, remember?"

"Oh yeah. I'm still half asleep, sorry."

"That's okay. But you're… you're in my time bubble with me."

"Does that mean I'm magic?"

"It might."

"But why?" she asks.

"I don't know. Maybe because you're in love with me or something."

"I never said I was in love with you."

"Neither did I. I just said maybe you are."

"Well maybe *you're* in love with *me.*"

"Maybe I am."

"Wait. Are you? In love with me?"

"Yes."

Her eyes widen and her smile spreads across her entire face. "Then that must be it. I'm magic because you're in love with me."

"Or because we're in love with each other?"

"No, I think it has everything to do with you being in love." But she says it with a playful tone, with a giggle just under her words.

"Morgan," I say through my grin.

"Nik."

We stare at each other for a good twenty seconds before she laughs.

"I'm magic because we're in love with each other," she says. "I'm in love with you."

"I'm in love with you too."

She presses into me and kisses me, and then stops and pulls back a little.

"What?" I ask.

"Your Santa suit is amazing."

"Oh." I look down at my red leather coat, lined with old, greyed fur, and then back at her. "Thanks. But I just call it a suit. Actually, I don't even call it that. It's my jacket."

"You weren't wearing this in the North Pole when I was there."

"Because I only need to wear this when I'm in the sleigh. It gets cold up there."

"Ah, okay, yes, that makes total sense."

"Come with me."

"What?" she asks.

"Come deliver presents with me. I'm almost done, it's just everything south of us and then back up north to the west."

"That actually sounds like a lot."

"Oh, but it'll be so much fun with you there. And I'll bring you back when we're done."

I can see her contemplating; her eyebrows raised a little as she bites her bottom lip.

"There's hot chocolate," I say.

"Oh. Well, if there's hot chocolate."

So Morgan comes with me, and I don't think I've ever had so much fun delivering presents before. It's even more fun than the first time I delivered presents with the reindeer, which I didn't think could be possible. But maybe it's because I have someone to share it with. But not just anyone, the person I'm in love with. The person I feel comfortable with, and feel like myself around when I didn't even know it was possible not to, is here with me in my magic bubble that used to only be for me. I love sharing this with her.

"Do you want to come into this house with me?" I ask, after we've started in a new town.

"What? How?"

I shrug. "I don't know, but you're in my time bubble with me, so I thought we could see if you can come into the house with me too. If we hold hands, maybe it'll work."

"Am I allowed?"

I let out a big, full belly laugh and throw my head back. "Of course you're allowed," I say. "Why wouldn't you be allowed?"

"I don't know. I'm not Santa! Isn't that against the rules?"

"Morgan," I say, tilting my head at her. "There are no rules."

She smiles, and looks down at my hand that I'm holding out to her. She grabs onto it and I close my fingers around hers.

"Wait," she says just above a whisper.

"Yes?"

"Will this make me throw up?"

"I hope not."

She shoves me in the shoulder with her free hand and I chuckle at her. "Shut up," she says playfully. "Will it feel like it did when Charlie teleported us?"

"No. It might be the distance that did that. And I still can't really wrap my head around how he has enough magic to travel that far. He was born with his magic though, and has had it for even longer than I have, so it makes sense, I guess. But we're just going a few feet below us, into their living room, so it won't feel the same. To me, it feels cozy and warm every time I do it. Like I can feel the magic in my veins."

"Like a CT scan?"

"I don't know what that is."

Morgan laughs a little and then nods. "Okay. Take me with you."

She tightens her grip on my hand, and I lean in and press my lips against hers as I take us into the house. The warmth fills me everywhere inside, and Morgan stumbles a little so I catch her against my chest.

"Whoa," she says, looking up at me.

"Okay?" I ask.

She nods, a smile taking up her entire face. "Yeah. That felt nothing like a CT scan."

I raise an eyebrow at her. "In a good way?"

"In a good way. It felt like I was made of magic."

She smiles against my mouth as I kiss her again, and when I pull away, she tugs me back in. Her arms wrap around me so I do the same with her, and in this moment, I've never felt so content. The glow of lights surround us and the feeling of magic in my veins heightens as I pull Morgan closer to me. The slow movements of her mouth on mine bring a calmness over me that I've never experienced. Everything is perfect.

She finally pulls back, slowly, like she wishes she didn't have to, and then slowly reaches up to my hat. She pulls it off my head and examines it in both her hands.

"This is really good quality," she says.

"Of course it's good quality, my elves made it."

"Yeah, but for some reason I was expecting everything you wore to be gimmicky."

"Why would it be gimmicky?"

"I don't know." She turns the hat around in her hands and runs her thumbs along the fur lining that matches the fur on my coat. "Everything I've seen of Santa has been cheap looking. They're just costumes."

"Yes, but this isn't a costume. These are my clothes."

"I know," she says with a bit of a laugh.

She hands it back to me, but instead of putting it on my head, I take her toque off and replace it with my hat. It's a little big on her, so I tilt it back and to the side a little so it doesn't fall in her eyes but will still keep her ears warm.

"It looks really good on you," I say.

She reaches up to touch it gently with her fingertips. "Thanks."

"Okay, I'm going to do my job now."

"Of course."

Morgan comes in with me to most of the houses on the rest of our journey, but sometimes she's fallen asleep and I don't want to wake her. Instead I'll give her a kiss on the nose, readjust my hat on her head, and come back to the sleigh as quickly as possible.

I like it when she's awake and wants to come in the houses with me, though. She exaggerates a fake gag every time I eat whatever is left of the food that was left out and then secretly munched on for pretend me. And yeah, I still put whatever I can in the stockings, and sometimes I leave a present under the tree. I never thought of leaving notes before, and writing the first two woke something up inside me that I don't want to put back to sleep. So I write a few more.

And I guess it's okay that the parents of today's world think I don't exist and do my job for me. Because kids think I exist, and I know I exist, and I can still do the job too, if I want. And I will. So if you ever wake up on Christmas morning and find a present that no one claims to have purchased and no one can figure out where it came from, it was probably from me.

Acknowledgements

The story that Morgan tells Olivia about Santa giving her a Hop 55 instead of a trampoline, but leaving a letter for her, is actually my story. That happened to me one year, when I was living in PEI, and it was one of the most magical things to get a handwritten letter from Santa outside of the normal letters he sends to everyone. This letter was special, and he wrote it in my living room! This was obviously not the only magical Christmas I've had, but it's one I will always remember. So thank you to my parents for lying to me as a child (ha) so that I could believe in magic just a little longer. Thank you for getting the dog to chew on the carrots we left out so that it looked like they got munched on by the reindeer (and then brought back to the living room after? Haha). Thank you for all that you did, and continue to do.

Thank you to Sarah Jane Wetelainen and Ray Sunshine, who helped edit drafts of this story and helped me make it the best that it can be.

Thank you to my place of work for having Christmas themed glass cloths in July; it was while drying glasses that I came up with the idea for the Gingerbread Elf to use instead of the other Elf that I'm not allowed to name. I do really like the Gingerbread Elves. I don't think I would have thought of it if I wasn't drying glasses with a cloth covered in gingerbread man cartoons.

Thank you again to Laura Kulson, my amazing cover artist, for making my vision come to life in a beautiful way. As usual, I'm completely obsessed with it.

And thank you to all my readers. I hope you enjoyed reading this as much as I enjoyed writing it!

Listen to the spotify playlist!
And don't worry, there are only two Christmas songs, and they're at the end so they're easily skippable if you don't like Christmas music. (They are the two best Christmas songs, though. Haha.)